This was simply a combination of chemicals, aligned to trigger these base instincts. Nothing more.

He would walk away as soon as this insanity was dispensed with. He spiked his fingers into her hair, angled her face up for a deeper kiss. A deeper taste.

And felt her hands on his chest. *Pushing him away.*

Maceo levered himself away, disbelief dripping ice and reality into his veins, reminding him of where he was. Of who he was.

"Stop. I... We can't," Faye said, her voice husky with arousal but firm enough to push him back another step.

While he'd been lost in her allure, the lights had come on. The last thing he wanted was to fuel the office rumor mill. Or was it something deeper? A reluctance for anyone to see what his instincts warned might be a growing obsession with this woman?

Maya Blake's hopes of becoming a writer were born when she picked up her first romance at thirteen. Little did she know her dream would come true! Does she still pinch herself every now and then to make sure it's not a dream? Yes, she does! Feel free to pinch her, too, via Twitter, Facebook or Goodreads! Happy reading!

Books by Maya Blake

Harlequin Presents

The Sultan Demands His Heir
His Mistress by Blackmail
An Heir for the World's Richest Man
The Sicilian's Banished Bride

Bound to the Desert King

Sheikh's Pregnant Cinderella

Conveniently Wed!

Crown Prince's Bought Bride

Passion in Paradise

Kidnapped for His Royal Heir

The Notorious Greek Billionaires

Claiming My Hidden Son
Bound by My Scandalous Pregnancy

Visit the Author Profile page
at Harlequin.com for more titles.

Maya Blake

THE COMMANDING ITALIAN'S CHALLENGE

HARLEQUIN®
PRESENTS®

ISBN-13: 978-1-335-40331-5

The Commanding Italian's Challenge

Copyright © 2020 by Maya Blake

This edition published by arrangement with Harlequin Books S.A.

For questions and comments about the quality of this book,
please contact us at CustomerService@Harlequin.com.

Harlequin Enterprises ULC
22 Adelaide St. West, 40th Floor
Toronto, Ontario M5H 4E3, Canada
www.Harlequin.com

Printed in U.S.A.

THE COMMANDING
ITALIAN'S CHALLENGE

CHAPTER ONE

FLY WITH THE ANGELS, mio dolce.

Maceo Fiorenti brushed a kiss over the petals of the single long-stemmed white rose, one of the specially cultivated ones imported from Holland that his wife—his *late* wife—had adored.

Carlotta had indulged in that extravagance, despite his gardener vowing he could recreate the genus right here in their Napoli home. She'd smilingly refused, insisting there was something special in having the flowers flown in twice weekly.

Of course Maceo had indulged her little whim. In their nine years of marriage he could count on the fingers of one hand the occasions when he'd said no to Carlotta Caprio-Fiorenti.

Those occasions had been triggered by her misguided attempts to make him into someone other than the man he saw in the mirror every day. A futile exercise to try to sway him from the path his actions had dictated for him. From a future that should rightly exact just penance for his actions. On those occasions, while it had pained him to see her heartache, he hadn't been swayed. How could he, when he didn't deserve a single breath he took, much less any semblance of happiness?

His lips twisted.

It was almost as if in those moments Carlotta had forgotten everything that had happened.

Had forgotten who he was. What he'd done.

Maceo Fiorenti—heir to a legacy he'd had no choice but to safeguard. Cursed with a destiny he couldn't walk away from because doing so would be the ultimate betrayal. He hadn't taken joy in showing Carlotta a glimpse of the demons that drove him. He'd simply reminded her that *he'd* been the cause of her ultimate heartache. *He'd* taken away the *famiglia* she'd held so dear.

There would be time enough to mourn this latest death—and its attendant layers of bitterness, shame and guilt—when he was far away from here.

For now, he had a legacy to protect. And as the sole remaining vanguard protect it he would, even if it took his last breath.

So what if in his darkest moments he questioned just why he was hanging on?

Because your conscience won't let you stop.

Casa di Fiorenti wasn't just his birthright. It was what his parents and his godfather, Luigi, had lived for. Died for. He owed it to them to keep their legacy alive. Even if he was dead inside. Even if he was haunted with the certainty that he would never enjoy a moment of happiness.

He allowed the tips of his fingers to brush one corner of the pristine white-and-gold coffin in one last, lingering caress.

Let go.

Jaw gritted, he released the flower. The heaviness in his heart grew but he pushed it down. He'd refused to acknowledge that this day was coming, that within months of her cancer diagnosis he'd have to face a future of truly being alone. Now he had no choice.

Maceo locked his knees against the ridiculous but serious threat of them giving way.

'Show no weakness.'

They were the words she'd spoken to him a little over a decade ago, when guilt had threatened to eat him alive, to rob him of the strength to rise from the ashes of his life. Words he'd absorbed, branded into his skin until they'd fused to his soul.

A deep breath and the moment of weakness rightly retreated.

He was *Maceo Fiorenti*. And, as much as it had been trifling sport for him and Carlotta to give the paparazzi fodder to gleefully splash gossip within the sordid pages of their tabloids for most of their married life, today wasn't a day for courting notoriety.

Carlotta was six feet under, reunited—as had been her final wish—with Luigi, her first husband, and Maceo's own parents. But for a twist of fate—ironically of his own making—Maceo, too, would be entombed in this family crypt alongside his family.

But he was very much alive. Despite the odds.

'A miracle', the papers had branded his return to the land of the living twelve years ago. Some had even called him *lucky*.

If only they knew the demons that haunted him. If only they had a taste of the guilt and regret that weighed him down.

Minutes passed as he stared down at the coffin. Minutes during which he felt eyes boring into his very skin. Board members. Acquaintances. Strangers. Sizing him up. Attempting to seek out his weaknesses.

They could try all they liked.

Half an hour later, once the *cardinale* had said his final blessing, Maceo turned his back on his family's final resting place and, ignoring everyone present, made his way across the sun-baked graveyard to his waiting car.

His driver sprang to attention, murmuring words of condolence Maceo didn't acknowledge as he opened the door.

Acknowledging them would mean accepting that he was alone in the world. Sure, as Carlotta's widower he would be saddled with a few dozen Caprios, who shamelessly laid claim to him in one in-law capacity or another. But flesh-and-blood-wise, with no siblings or extended family to speak of, he was the sole remaining Fiorenti.

Alone.

He slid into the back seat, plucked the shades from his eyes and tossed them aside. Exhaling loudly, he massaged the bridge of his nose, willing the tension headache away.

'You wish to return to the villa, *signor*?' his driver asked, disturbing the momentary eerie quiet.

Maceo opened his mouth to confirm that he did,

but at the last moment shook his head. Why prolong the inevitable? It was Friday afternoon, and most of his staff had been given the day off to pay their respects to Carlotta, but there was work to be done.

And, no, his reluctance to return to the villa in Capri had nothing to do with the empty *salones* and corridors awaiting him, newly devoid of Carlotta's presence.

'Take me to the helipad. I'm returning to the office.'

With a nod, the older man drove him away from his wife's graveside and the crowd of Napoli's high society, all vying to see him do something worth gossiping about.

Maceo barely registered the helicopter ride that deposited him two streets away from the temporary headquarters of Casa di Fiorenti.

When she'd known the end was near, Carlotta had requested to be closer to the Capri summer home she'd shared with Luigi and Maceo's parents. He'd willingly relocated his company from Rome to the sprawling eighteenth-century building overlooking Naples Harbour. The building where, predictably, two dozen paparazzo now waited, rabid, with long lenses and sharp questions the moment they spotted him.

He slid his sunglasses back on, allowed himself the faintest sigh.

'Maceo! What would Carlotta think of you returning to work even before she's in the ground?'

'Maceo, any plans to make your brothers-in-law directors now Carlotta's gone?'

'Maceo, when will you make an announcement about who will fill your late wife's shoes?'

Teeth gritted, he charged forward, leaving his bodyguards to deal with the throng. It bemused him that they continued to throw questions at him when he never answered. Did they truly expect him to divulge all his dark, guilty secrets simply because they demanded it? Especially when the games he and Carlotta had played with them had been meant to hide the biggest, most terrible secret of them all?

He shoved at the heavy door separating his empire from the gossip-hungry mob, his gut tightening at the reminder of the other bombshell Carlotta had thrown at his feet a week ago. He had to compliment her timing. She'd known he'd be incapable of challenging her in any way. That because of that heavy boulder of guilt he carried he would grant her wishes, regardless of the shock and fury boiling in his stomach at her news.

But, while he'd agreed to honour Carlotta's final requests, he'd withheld how he intended to proceed. That was between him and the woman he'd hadn't known existed until a week ago.

Luigi had been previously married, albeit briefly, to an Englishwoman. A woman who'd had a daughter. Another secret his parents and godfather had kept from him.

Maceo's gut tightened with fresh bitterness. They'd blithely ignored the *famiglia* they'd purportedly valued and burdened him with honouring their wishes.

More than that, Maceo had also discovered that Casa di Fiorenti, the confectionery empire his grandparents and parents had built thirty years ago, which *he'd* turned into a multi-billion-euro conglomerate, didn't belong wholly and exclusively to him. That a slice—albeit a very small slice, which he probably wouldn't miss if it broke off and fell into the Mediterranean Sea, but was nevertheless *his* by right—belonged to a faceless, grasping gold-digger, already sharpening her claws in anticipation of a hefty payday.

A woman named Faye Bishop.

Carlotta had kept tabs on her from afar over the years, and reached out in the past few months without much success.

And now Maceo was supposed to tolerate this woman for a stretch of time, fulfilling Carlotta's last wish.

Anger intensified as he stalked into his private lift.

Faye Bishop had dangled a promise to his dying wife she'd had no intention of keeping. Yet she'd found the time to email his lawyers and accept their invitation to attend the will reading next week.

A dark anticipatory smile curved his lips as he stabbed the button for his office.

Faye Bishop might have succeeded in pulling the wool over Carlotta's eyes.

Maceo would savour teaching her a lesson she would never forget.

Faye resisted the urge to glance at the sleek, near-silent clock, gracefully sweeping its way towards noon. For one thing, it would only confirm that just twenty seconds had passed since she last checked. For another, it wouldn't dissipate the weird sensation of being watched.

Although, thinking about it, it wasn't that strange. Every wall in the stunning conference room she sat in was made of smoky glass, in sharp contrast to the shiny clear surfaces of the vast table and chairs, the cabinets and the sci-fi-looking communication system poised in the middle of the table. The smoked glass was most likely a two-way mirror, allowing her to be gawped at and gossiped about without being any the wiser.

Besides feeling a world away from the remote Devon farm she'd travelled from yesterday, Faye knew her feeling of being a fish out of water extended beyond the sensation prickling her skin. After all, she'd put considerable effort into resembling a fish out of water. So, really, she couldn't fault anyone for gawping. In fact…

She aimed a look at the centre of the widest glass wall and smiled.

Imagining she'd startled one or even several people with her *you can't intimidate me* smile, she relaxed as a layer of tension eased away.

The bulk of her anxiety remained, though. It was a different sensation from that generated by the clutch of tabloid journalists downstairs, who'd pounced on her the moment she'd stepped out of the taxi, but just as unnerving.

More than once in the last hour she'd considered walking out.

If only she hadn't answered her phone all those weeks ago. If only she hadn't made Carlotta Caprio that promise. One she now felt obligated to keep after learning of the older woman's death.

You don't owe her or Luigi's family anything. You should leave them in the past, where they belong.

Her smile died. It was too late. Luigi was gone, taking all Faye's bewildered questions to his grave. And now his wife was dead too.

Really, she had no business being here, grasping at straws and hoping that maybe someone had answers for her—

Her thoughts stalled as the door to the conference room sprang open. Her notions of leaving evaporated, replaced by different questions as she froze.

Questions like what the identity of the man who'd entered was—because he looked *nothing* like a lawyer. Sure, he'd aced the ruthless cut-throat demeanour well enough to evoke images of sharpened blades and sharks' teeth. But there was something else. Something barely contained, something electrifying that gripped her and tightened its hold as seconds ticked by.

Seconds during which she was aware she was gawping. With eyes wide and her mouth possibly hanging open. Seconds during which she couldn't summon a single command her brain was willing to follow. Like blink. Swallow.

Slow down her runaway heartbeat.

The fact that this non-lawyer seemed equally fascinated with her was neither here nor there. Faye was aware that she attracted dumbfounded looks wherever she went. Partly because of her eclectic clothing. Possibly because of the profusion of hennaed flowers climbing up her right arm. But mostly because of the uniqueness of her hair.

She was pleased she resisted the sudden urge to reach up and smooth down the silver, lilac and purple tresses knotted haphazardly atop her head, especially when the stranger's gaze rose to rest there.

What she *wasn't* pleased about was her inability to look away. Her utter, almost helpless absorption with him. She shouldn't, *couldn't* be this affected.

Yes, he was indescribably handsome—enough to give every Roman god a run for his money and easily come out on top.

Yes, he commanded the very air around the

room, as if harnessing it to power his godlike form and leaving none for mere mortals.

But liaisons and connections with members of the opposite sex, after that single traumatic event with Matt two years ago, had been permanently delisted from her life.

Aware that her whole body was clenched in peculiar expectancy, as if awaiting some sort of trigger to bring her back to life, she attempted to drag herself free of his forcefield.

A throat was cleared, disrupting the charged atmosphere.

'*Signor...*' A man, who thankfully did resemble a lawyer, spoke in low tones from behind the formidable figure.

The formal address was the only thing Faye understood. The rest of the hushed Italian buzzed in her brain as more men filed into the room, leaving *him* at the door, still blatantly staring at her.

The team of four sat across from Faye at the gleaming conference table, each casting surreptitious glances at various parts of her body. Had she not been wholly enthralled by the man who now sauntered forward with an animal grace that belied his towering height and size to settle into the seat directly opposite hers, she might have been amused.

But this wasn't a jaunt to the pub. Or one of those bring-your-own-instrument-for-a-singalong gatherings her mother spontaneously threw when she was lucid.

She was here because Luigi Caprio had left an indelible mark on her, with the kind of familial love she'd never experienced before, then exited her life without explanation, leaving a worse wreck than he'd found and two lives spiralling out of control.

Faye tried to numb herself against the never healed pain, raked open by Carlotta Caprio.

'How very good of you to make it, Miss Bishop,' the man drawled, once he'd settled his sleek, animal-like frame into the chair, his eyes—which she noted were a rich tawny gold—spearing into her.

Unlike his words, his expression was anything but cordial. For some reason this man despised her.

Her hackles rose, along with a bone-deep shame. Dear God, did he *know*? Had Luigi done the unthinkable and shared Faye and her mother's secret with this man? Would he have been so cruel?

Dread crawled across her skin even as she reassured herself that it didn't matter. Once she left this place she needn't set eyes on this enigmatic man, or any of Luigi's kin, ever again.

She raised her chin. 'I made a promise to Carlotta,' she replied.

It was a promise the other woman had had no business demanding of her. And yet she had. And, because of the curse of the unknown that had always plagued Faye, she'd given in.

The man's lips twisted. 'Ah, *si*… A promise to attend a will reading but not to pay your last respects?'

Her spine snapped straight at his contempt. 'For

your information, Mr...whoever-you-are, Carlotta didn't tell me she was ill. Not until our last conversation three weeks ago. After that I didn't think it was appropriate to just...turn up. Not when I was a stranger to her.'

'And yet here you are now,' he said, his deep, rumbling voice and disturbingly attractive accent stretching out the words. Deepening their barbed meaning. Thickening their accusation.

Finally her muscles obeyed the commands she'd shrieked at her brain and lent her enough strength to stand. She pushed back her chair and grabbed the hobo bag she'd tossed on the floor beside her. 'Save your accusations. I was already thinking this was a mistake before you walked in. You've just confirmed that I shouldn't have come here. Let's not waste each other's time any longer. I'm leaving.'

'I'm afraid it's not going to be that easy, Miss Bishop.'

Her fingers tightened around the strap of her bag. 'What isn't? And, seriously, are you going to introduce yourself, like a normal person, or is your identity some mystery I'm supposed to unravel to get to the next level of why I'm here?'

More than one lawyer gasped. Her impression of stepping deeper into a minefield heightened as the stranger's gaze swept downwards in a slow, languid journey from her face, her throat, her chest, to rest on the three-inch gap between her midriff-baring pink top and the waistband of her bohemian ankle-length, patchwork skirt. There it rested, partly in disbelief, partly with a sizzling indecipherable look that sent gooseflesh skittering over her skin.

'Sit down,' he commanded after an aeon, his voice barely above a murmured rumble.

Faye couldn't, because the look in his eyes had paralysed her again. And as he continued to watch her, other sensations crept in, adding to the chaos. Weakness swept through her frame. Her breasts began to tingle, shooting warnings that her bra-less state was about to become glaringly obvious.

To counteract that impending discomfort, Faye folded her arms and aimed a glare across the table. 'Why?' she asked, very much aware that his interest had shifted to the inked flowers decorating her arm. That he looked even more…intrigued.

Intrigue didn't last long before his gaze hardened.

'Because I'm about to lay a few facts on you, Miss Bishop. Contrary to what you think you're here for, my revelations will far exceed your wildest dreams. Unfortunately for you, those dreams come with strings. Of course once I'm done you can still insist on taking this dubious high road you're posturing about. And should you decide to relinquish your inheritance—'

'My *inheritance*? What inheritance?' Surprise made her voice cringingly squeaky.

'Sit down and I will tell you,' he instructed again.

Shock propelled her legs to obey. She sank into the seat, and in the moment before he spoke again her gaze darted to the lawyers, noting their solemn looks.

'Now, let's pretend you *really* have no clue who I am—'

'I don't. I'm not sure why that's so unfathomable to you, but I haven't the foggiest idea who you are.'

He stared at her for another long, tight stretch. Then he leaned forward. 'My name is Maceo Fiorenti.'

The surname was familiar. Painfully so. She'd blocked it out of her life—albeit unsuccessfully, because of its sheer size and success—because of its association with Luigi.

'I'm assuming that you're in some way connected to Casa di Fiorenti?'

The lawyers exchanged stunned glances.

'You could say that. But I am also... I *was* also connected to Carlotta.'

In her emails, Carlotta had signed off as Carlotta Caprio-Fiorenti. Faye hadn't given the Fiorenti attachment much thought. Now she did, with a peculiar feeling dragging in her stomach.

The man across the conference table was too old to be Carlotta's son, so he could only be—

Faye felt her jaw gaping again and caught herself. 'You're Carlotta's *husband*?' Why did that knowledge send sharp pangs through her chest? 'But you're—' She stopped, bit her lip to cut off the rest of her words.

One masculine brow lifted in mocking query. 'I'm what, Miss Bishop? Too young? A *toy boy*, as you refer to it in your country? Don't be afraid to speak up. You won't be saying anything the media haven't attempted to dissect a million ways.'

Heat flared up her neck, since she'd been about to say exactly that. Carlotta had been in her late-fifties, while Maceo Fiorenti looked at least thirty years younger.

But this wasn't why she was here. Heck, she was still in the dark as to the reason for her presence in this room. With this man who fascinated her far more than she should allow him to.

'Your relationship with Carlotta is none of my business, I'm sure. And now we're properly introduced, perhaps you could enlighten me as to why I'm here?'

'I'm CEO of Casa di Fiorenti and one hundred percent shareholder of this company. Or at least I thought I was until a week ago.'

Faye frowned. 'What does that mean?'

He leaned forward, and every instinct urged her to retreat. She held her ground. Because to appear weak would be to grant him victory.

'It means that my late wife informed me that Luigi—I'm assuming you do know who *he* is?' he drawled.

She steeled herself against the pain that should have dulled after all this time, but curiously hadn't. 'Of course.'

'Meraviglioso,' he said sarcastically. 'My late wife informed me that Luigi had requested that,

should he pass away before you turned twenty-five, Carlotta pass on a bequest in her will or when you reached that age. I take it you celebrated your birthday recently?'

Faye nodded absently. 'Three months ago.' Then she caught her breath. 'That's when Carlotta first contacted me. But…why didn't she tell me?'

'Did you give her the chance? Or did you repeatedly rebuff her attempts to reach out to you?' he asked.

She suspected he knew the answer. Guilt flushed through her, but she refused to cower. 'I had my reasons.'

Pain. Betrayal. The stigma of shame that had never gone away. The anxiety of not knowing why Luigi had left and never looked back but had seemingly kept tabs on her.

'No one can love an abomination like you…'

Matt's words echoed in her head, intensifying the anguish. In truth, she'd succeeded in partially silencing the *why* of Luigi's desertion until those damning words. Now she feared she would never move on. Not until she knew if Luigi had felt the same way.

'Ah, but you didn't feel strongly enough about those reasons to stay away because you'd "made a promise", *si*?'

Far from being needled by his determination to get under her skin, Faye forced herself to sit back. To smile and shrug. 'It's obvious you think I have an agenda, so let's dispense with the rhetorical questions and get on with it, shall we? I have…' She made a show of checking the time on the clock before settling her gaze somewhere over his shoulder. From the corner of her eye, she saw his jaw clench. 'I have about half a day's sightseeing before I go back to my hotel.'

Terse silence greeted her. His tawny gaze compelled her. Unable to resist, Faye found herself looking into eyes that held what looked like grief. She couldn't be sure because it had disappeared a second later. What didn't disappear was the guilt that assailed her.

Regardless of what had happened in the past, the anguish Luigi's desertion had caused her and her mother, this man had buried his wife only a few days ago. At the very least she owed him a modicum of compassion.

She opened her mouth, but before she could retract her flippant words he spoke.

'As the executor of Carlotta's will, it falls to me to inform you that, through your stepfather's bequest, you now own a quarter of one percent of a share in Casa di Fiorenti. Signor Abruzzo, kindly inform Miss Bishop what that means in monetary terms.'

One of the lawyers cleared his throat and flipped open a folder while Maceo lounged in his seat, all panther-like grace and piercing eyes, content to stare her down.

The effect of that stare caused her to miss the be-

ginning of the lawyer's heavily accented speech. Forcing herself to concentrate, Faye caught the last of it.

'...at the last financial audit, Casa di Fiorenti
was valued at five point six billion euros. Which
makes the value of your inheritance approximately
fourteen million euros.'

CHAPTER TWO

MACEO WATCHED THE strange creature's full lush lips fall open. Then immediately cursed himself for that unwelcome observation.

Her lips could rival Cupid's bow. So what?

Per l'amor di Dio, she had purple and silver hair! There were other colours in there, too. She was garbed in hippie clothes and one arm was decorated with flowers. Lush lips and dramatically eye-catching figure or not, she belonged on the set of some fairy-tale movie, not in the corporate offices of his billion-euro empire.

So what if her skin was the most flawless he'd ever seen and her indigo eyes seemed almost too good to be true...the most alluring he'd ever looked into?

He'd buried Carlotta just days ago. And, while their marriage hadn't been quite conventional, he owed her the respect of not listing adjectives to describe the shape of another woman's—

'You're joking!'

Her words refocused him. Infused him with the iciness and distance and gravity he should be clinging to—especially now, when Casa di Fiorenti should be his sole occupation.

'Of course I am. Because of course I would choose now, a few days after burying my wife, to make a tasteless joke about her wishes.'

She had the decency to flush. But her contrition lasted only a handful of seconds. 'My reaction wasn't intended as an insult. This really is the last thing I expected.'

'*Is* it? Truly, Miss Bishop?' Maceo didn't bother to hide his scepticism. He didn't intend to hide anything from her. Secrets were what had eroded his family's foundations.

'Yes, it is. *Mr Fiorenti*,' she snapped, her peculiar eyes sparking.

'Then do as you intended before. Refuse it and leave.'

Curiously fascinated, he watched her tilt her head and return his stare. Sunlight danced off the multicoloured strands of her hair and Maceo forced his gaze to remain on her face, attempted to stave off the effect of this woman's presence on his senses.

He'd stopped in his tracks when he spotted her through the glass, certain he was hallucinating. And even after becoming aware that he was drawing the attention of his executive staff Maceo had been unable to move. He'd been stunned at the curious sensations cascading through him—the most startling and damning being the ferocious pounding in his groin. A torrid and wholly unwelcome reminder, today of all days, that he was a man. With primal needs. Needs long and ruthlessly denied because he didn't *deserve* to have them satisfied. Needs denied in order to achieve his goals. To hold on to what his parents had devoted themselves to.

He hadn't survived hell to fall prey to a passing fascination with this pixie-like creature.

'Your lawyers appear uncomfortable with that idea. Why is that, Mr Fiorenti?' she enquired softly, then held up the arm decorated with hennaed flowers. 'Wait—don't answer that. I'll hazard a wild guess, shall I? They're fidgeting because you're not allowed to tell me to do that.' She glanced at the lawyer who had spoken. 'Am I right, sir?'

His lawyer—damn the man—squirmed guiltily. 'That is open to interpretation, but broadly speaking...*si*—'

The blinding, dare-filled smile she'd flashed at the window as he'd stood staring at her from behind the veil of glass—the smile that had stopped every red-blooded employee within the vicinity—curved into view again, complete with groin-tightening dimples, cutting off his lawyer's words.

Maceo's insides dipped in a mixture of arousal and guilt that made his fist curl on the table. Her gaze swung to his hand and the smile dimmed. He frowned, unsure why the look in her eyes disturbed him. He visibly relaxed, but even though her smile remained, it lacked...*something*.

Something he wasn't going to concern himself with.

He leaned forward, eager to get this meeting over and done with. Faye Bishop wasn't the only inconvenience Carlotta had left behind for him to deal with. There was added the nuisance of her brothers.

'The bequest must be administered. But here's the stinger, Miss Bishop. I have the power to add my own stipulations.'

Her smile evaporated completely. 'What?'

'Your reluctance to engage with Carlotta gave her pause. In her will she's given me the power either to make you a very rich woman today or…' He sat back, let his silence speak.

Her lips firmed. 'Or make me jump through hoops for something I had no idea about and didn't want in the first place?'

Maceo delivered a derisive smile. 'Indulge me, then. Get up and walk out. Prove you mean to refuse it.'

He was confident that she wouldn't. No one in their right mind would walk away from such a—

Shock reverberated through him when she rose again. Her indigo eyes effortlessly pierced the layers of his calm until Maceo wasn't sure whether he was breathing in or out. Whether he was going to jump up to stop her leaving or remain seated and watch her go.

The latter.

He most definitely wasn't going to stop her.

She took one step, then another. Despite her tasteless clothes, her grace was unmistakable, and her hips swayed beneath her sweeping skirt with a raw sensuality that made Maceo shift in his seat. And stare.

She reached the door and grabbed the handle. Tension coiled tight within him. Realising his fingers were drumming on the table, he killed the action just as she turned to spear him with a reproving look that would have levelled a lesser man. A man who *hadn't* committed the sins he had and emerged with the demons he fought every day.

'I came here because I thought that after all this time Luigi had provided the answers I've been seeking all these years. I see now it was a waste of time.'

Maceo sent his lawyer a warning glance as the older man opened his mouth. Carlotta's other request, over and above the financial bequest, had been specific—the delivery of a letter addressed to Faye Bishop. He didn't know whether it would provide the answers she claimed to seek, but Maceo knew he would only deliver it when he was absolutely sure of her motives.

'I'm sorry for your loss, Mr Fiorenti. But I hope I never see or hear from you ever again.'

She walked out, leaving astounded silence behind.

'Did she…? Did that really just happen?' one lawyer asked, stunned.

Maceo refused to acknowledge his own astonishment. She had to be playing a game. What she didn't know was that he was an expert at games.

He'd been playing them for the better part of a decade with the paparazzi, keeping them distracted so they didn't dig and uncover his family's secrets. The same games he had played with those board members who deemed him weak.

As if on cue, two of his opponents walked in. Stefano and Francesco Castella—Carlotta's older brothers. Maceo's life had taken a fateful turn the night his parents and his godfather had perished, but these two remained a constant reminder that, besides the secrets that had eventually shattered his family, lies and greed were a menace he also had to deal with.

He neutralised his features into a mask of indifference even as his gaze flicked to the door. What had Faye Bishop meant? What had his godfather done to her?

And how did I not know Luigi had a stepdaughter?

Realising his thoughts were cartwheeling, Maceo pushed the subject of the ethereal Faye Bishop to the back of his mind.

'I didn't realise we were letting in strays off the street these days. Who *was* that curious woman?' Stefano asked.

'She's none of your concern,' Maceo answered, a little taken aback by the bite in his own voice.

Stefano smiled his oily smile. 'Ah, but I'm a board member. That makes everything my concern.'

Maceo swallowed a growl. There was another reason he needed to deal with Faye Bishop. That fraction of a share was the only thing preventing him from having absolute power over the board. However measly, it might be the difference between ridding himself of Stefano and Francesco—who'd made Carlotta's life a living hell until Maceo had stepped in—and enduring their unpalatable presence.

'You're here to discuss your sister's personal affairs. That woman isn't any part of that,' he said.

Stefano shrugged. 'I was simply being civil to pass the time—'

'You don't know the meaning of the word *civil*, so don't insult me.'

Francesco's gaze narrowed. 'Watch your tone, *figlio*. We not only managed this company while you lay incapacitated in a hospital bed and Carlotta was uselessly wringing her hands, we *allowed* you to marry our sister—'

'I was under the impression that decision was entirely *ours*,' Maceo inserted calmly. 'I'm sure that's why we married without informing either of you.'

Stefano slapped his palm on the table. '*Ascoltami*—'

'No. *You* listen,' Maceo interrupted, his patience gossamer-thin. 'Carlotta was too kind-hearted to tell you that she despised both of you. You made her life hell when she married Luigi and you treated her contemptibly at every opportunity until she made you rich. Now she's gone, and I harbour no such inclination. Your positions in this company are secure…for now. Don't push me or your circumstances will change very quickly.'

He rose from the table, itching to be away from this room. He assured himself that the other reason he was so eager to leave had nothing to do with accessing his security team to verify that Faye Bishop had truly left the building.

Casting one last dismissive glance at the brothers, he added, 'Your sister left you some personal effects. I'll leave Signor Abruzzo to apprise you of them.'

He left the room to ringing silence.

One step out the door and he was retrieving his phone. His assistant answered on the first ring. 'Get Security to track down the woman who was just here. Her name is Faye Bishop. I want her back here *pronto*—'

'There's no need, *signor*. Miss Bishop is waiting in your office.'

Maceo slid his phone back into his pocket and told himself the rush of heat through his veins *wasn't* anticipation. Just as he'd dealt with Carlotta's brothers, he would simply deal with another loose end.

With every bone in her body Faye wished she'd had the nerve to keep walking once she'd decided to reject Carlotta's bequest. But…

Pride goes before a fall.

And hers had been one prideful act she'd known, even as it was enfolding, she'd have to go back on. Because, ultimately, this wasn't about her.

It was about her mother.

It was about every woman who needed vital assistance.

Every victim who could use some support to get back on their feet.

She'd made it as far as the breathtaking steel, marble and glass atrium on the ground floor before good sense had kicked in. Thank goodness the receptionist there had accepted her explanation that she had unfinished business with Signor Fiorenti and allowed her to return to the top floor. Surprisingly, she'd been directed to the CEO's office, instead of the conference room, and here she'd been cooling her heels for the last half-hour, pondering the consequences of her hasty decision.

Had she, with a few emotive words, ruined her chances of helping countless women in need? Would the formidable man who had informed her of her inheritance give her the chance to take back her decision?

A hot little tremor shook through her at the thought of facing him again.

Maceo Fiorenti seemed the unforgiving sort who would hold a grudge. Perhaps even enjoy taunting her. Hell, he'd been bristling with rancour before they'd exchanged a word. It was clear he saw her as undeserving of this inheritance. Which meant she had a fight on her hands...

The heavy opaque glass door opened and, as if summoned by her frenzied imagination, he walked in. Faye jumped up from where she'd perched on the edge of the sofa in the vast, dramatically grey-and-glass corner office.

He barely spared her a glance. Crossing the room, he shrugged off his jacket and tossed it towards a sleek-looking coatrack. It landed perfectly, she was sure, but Faye wasn't paying attention to the jacket. Her eyes were riveted on the play of sleek muscles; her mouth drying as she took in the sheer breadth of his shoulders, the sculpted back, trim waist and the hint of washboard abs.

His body was in pristine condition, honed to perfection, with not a single ounce of superfluous flesh on display. Coupled with his height and jaw-dropping features, it was sinful how magnificent he was.

But she wasn't here to admire his physique, enthralling as it was. She was here to reverse the damage she'd done.

She swallowed and opened her mouth, just as he looked up and spoke, his eyes freezing her in place.

'I'm not sure whether to be disappointed at this backtracking or to praise you for the humble pie you're clearly willing to eat by returning.'

So much for hoping he'd let it go.

She forced a shrug. 'You can be both, as long as you hear me out.'

'*Bene.* Let's hear another impassioned speech you don't really mean.'

Faye swallowed her irritation. 'I was too hasty. I shouldn't have said what I said.'

He flicked her a dismissive glance, his lips twisting in faint amusement. 'I have already gathered that much. The question is why did you say it?'

'I meant it at the time. I expected something else when I came here.'

Some small indication that Luigi hadn't found her an abomination. That the harrowing sadness she still glimpsed in her mother's eyes when she was too drugged up to conceal her emotions wasn't the reason Luigi had turned his back on them.

That got Maceo's attention. 'What exactly did you expect from a woman you ignored for weeks?'

'I didn't expect anything from your…from Carlotta.'

Faye wasn't sure why the word *wife* stuck in her throat. Perhaps because she found it difficult to imagine this man married to Carlotta. She grimaced inwardly at the sexist thought. For all she knew they'd been a perfect match, wildly in love.

That curious dart returned, sharper than before. She doubled her efforts to suppress it.

'I wanted to know why Luigi…my stepfather…'

She stopped, unwilling to divulge the depth of her hurt to a stranger. Even if that stranger had, until recently, been married to the widow of her stepfather.

Faye shook her head. The whole thing was confounding. 'When your lawyers mentioned Carlotta had left something for me, I wasn't expecting it to be shares in Luigi's company.'

His eyes hardened. 'It is a fraction of a single share.'

She shrugged. 'Yes. Whatever...'

'There you go again—pretending you don't give a damn about the fortune that's landed in your lap. You're going to have to do better than this flippant performance, Miss Bishop.'

'It's not a performance. I care about the inheritance, obviously, or I wouldn't have returned. I just wanted something...*more*.'

An expression flickered through his eyes, but he veiled his features with the simple act of glancing down. The avoidance lasted only seconds before he was back to dissecting her with laser-like precision.

'Why now? He's been dead for over a decade.'

She wasn't fooled by his silky tone. Suspicion rolled off him in radioactive waves. Her heart slowed to a dull, painful thud, and she was bracingly aware in that moment of the dark stain she carried. The reason she strove to live her life in light, lest the darkness overwhelm her.

'I thought perhaps he hadn't wanted to say whatever he needed to say to my face.'

Again something intangible flickered in his eyes, lifting the hairs on her nape. Again the look disappeared, taking with it that tiny seedling of hope.

'My godfather was many things, but he wasn't a man who lived in fear of little girls. What do you believe he needed to say to you that he couldn't when he was alive?' he asked.

Faye shook her head, her insides locking tight around her secret. 'That's between him and me. Or not, as it turns out, since there's nothing besides this fraction of a share you're so annoyed about.'

Bleak amusement glinted in his eyes. 'You think that's what I am? *Annoyed?*'

'You certainly don't seem joyful about it—'

'Perhaps because we both know you don't deserve it, and nor did you do anything to earn it,' he sliced in.

'Whereas *you* have?' Faye wasn't sure why she felt the urge to needle him. 'Correct me if I'm wrong, but aren't you the silver spoon recipient of what Luigi built?'

His face hardened into an iron mask, his eyes livid flames of displeasure. 'Permit me to correct that misconception. My grandfather started this company with one shop here in Napoli. My father took over when he was twenty-one and expanded the company into Europe. It was my family's hard work that got it off the ground. Luigi's contribution was immeasurable, of course, but he didn't come on board until much later. As to your assumption that I've merely ridden on the coat-tails of my forebears—I'll leave you to discover how wrong you are in your own time. You've already wasted enough of mine. Do you want to discuss how you will justify your inheritance or waste more time dispensing insults?'

Faye realised just how much she'd wounded his pride by his haughty expression. Since she knew the company was now a billion-euro luxury confectionery brand, Faye didn't need telling that *he* had been responsible for that meteoric expansion.

She swallowed and attempted to corral her turbulent emotions. 'I… I'd like to discuss this. What do I need to do?'

He regarded her for several seconds and, had she been invited to guess, she would've said he was disappointed she hadn't taken a third option and thrown his offer back in his face. But then that peculiar gleam entered his eyes again. Almost as if he was relishing this skirmish. And why wouldn't he? Hadn't she just presented him with the perfect opportunity to exact his pound of flesh for her insults?

With growing apprehension, she watched him stroll around to perch on the corner of his vast glass desk. The motion drew her attention to his muscled thighs, to the high polish of his shoes and to the stern reminder that she was in the rarefied company of one of the world's youngest billionaires. His expression suggested she should count herself lucky that a man of his calibre was giving her the time of day.

He could easily throw her out. Why didn't he?

Because he'd made a promise to Carlotta? The wife he'd adored…?

'Miss Bishop?'

She started. His sharp tone indicated that she'd missed a chunk of what he'd said. 'I'm sorry, can you repeat that?'

His lips—comprising a thin upper and a surprisingly full and sensual lower, which alarmingly evoked lustful forbidden thoughts—firmed. 'I invited you, once again, to sit down.'

She frowned. He had a thing about ordering her to be seated. Was it merely a power play or…?

'Am I boring you or are you under the misconception that I appreciate flighty females?' he rasped, his accent thickening with irritation.

'You're aren't—and I'm not. I'm just trying to wrap my head around all of this. Haven't you ever had a bombshell dropped on you?'

Bleakness dulled his eyes before he blinked it away. 'More times that you will ever have the misfortune to encounter, I'm sure.'

She sat down and dragged her gaze from his to the painting behind his desk, pretending to study what looked like a priceless masterpiece as she fought the urge to inform him how wrong he was. How no one in the world should have to bear the burden of the bombshells she'd had dropped on her.

Abruptly he rose, crossed the room and seated himself directly opposite her, forcing her to focus on him. Not that it was any hardship. He was the epitome of a hot flame on a cold, dark night, drawing a hapless moth to its doom. She stared, taking in the vibrancy of his olive skin, the pronounced jut of his Adam's apple and the steady pulse beating at his throat.

An unfettered urge to stroke her fingers over that spot took Faye by surprise, making her swallow a gasp. Maceo's eyes narrowed, then conducted a sizzling scrutiny of his own before resting on her suddenly tingling mouth.

She wasn't sure how long they stayed locked in that tight, breath-robbing capsule. His phone's ping made her jump, releasing her from the spell.

Maceo glanced down for a moment before his gaze returned to hers. The heat had receded, and in its place was cool regard. 'Just so there's no misinterpreting the information, I'll have my lawyers provide you with a copy of Carlotta's will once we're done here. Your inheritance will be handed over at my discretion. And I've decided, Miss Bishop, that you need to appreciate where the money came from. Perhaps once you experience the hard work and sacrifice that went into your windfall, you won't be as flippant about it.'

Faye frowned. 'I told you—that was just shock. It wasn't my intention to cause offence.'

'Then prove it. I am not simply going to hand over the share. Carlotta didn't want me to and, after meeting you, I am certainly not inclined to.'

'What's that supposed to mean—after meeting me? You barely know me!'

The moment he leaned back in his seat she knew her response was what he'd angled for all along. And she'd walked straight into his trap.

'Here's your chance to rectify that, then. Prove that this bequest means more to you than just money.'

'How? Do you wish me to commission a plaque in Luigi and Carlotta's honour? Sign my name in blood? Maybe get a tattoo on my skin?'

He shrugged, as if they were discussing the weather, but Faye instinctively knew his every word so far had been calculated to gain this result.

'Nothing so dramatic. My request is simple. Walk in their shoes for a time. You will stay in Italy, immerse yourself in Casa di Fiorenti. Show a little appreciation for what Luigi spent his life building. When I'm satisfied, you'll receive your inheritance.'

Faye gripped the armrests of her chair, unsure whether to be shocked or amused. His face was deadly serious, and his eyes warned her to plot her next move wisely or prepare to lose.

'I have obligations. I can't just abandon them to come here and jump through hoops for you.'

He shrugged, distracting her with those incredible shoulders. 'Then by all means leave. Carlotta has granted me a flexible timescale of up to five years. Perhaps she believed you wouldn't be so quick to turn up once she was gone? Let my assistant know when you think you'll be available during the next five years and I'll endeavour to make some time in my schedule for you.'

Her fingers dug into the expensive leather as he sauntered back to his desk, opened a file and proceeded to ignore her.

Faye forced her jaw to unlock. 'That doesn't work for me.'

He didn't look up. 'Then we're at an impasse, Miss—'

'My name is Faye. I'd prefer you use it instead of that barbed formality designed to put me in my place—wherever you deem that to be. Believe me, I'm very aware of our differences, and I promise I won't tell if you come down a step or two from your lofty perch.'

He relaxed deeper into his seat, taking a stance that she was learning meant keener speculation, a deadlier attack. 'What do you do for a living... Faye?'

The effect of his voice uttering her name was unexpectedly visceral. Disturbing enough to double her pulse rate and make her aware of every inch of her skin.

'Why do I think you already know the answer to that question?'

He offered a cunning smile. 'Carlotta mentioned that you spend your time on a farm in... Where is it, exactly?'

Her heart missed a beat, but she fought to keep her expression neutral as she wondered what else Carlotta had told him about her. Had she mentioned her mother at all?

'It's a place in southwest England, in Devon.'

His gaze wandered lazily over her clothes. 'Some sort of hippie commune, I gather?' he drawled.

'It's a little more than that.'

A lot more, in fact. It was a vital place for respite and support. But she wasn't going to elaborate just for him to disparage her. Or, heaven forbid, decipher why it was that her mother lived there and *she* devoted every minute she could spare to it.

'And what do you do there?'

'I'm a social worker by profession, but I currently volunteer there.'

Since her employment contract had ended, and there were no funds to hire her even on a temporary basis, Faye had been offering her services for free at New Paths Centre while she looked for another job. As much as she hated to admit it, Carlotta's bequest would do financial wonders for New Paths and also fund other much-needed centres— a project she'd been pouring her energy into since she'd left university, with little to no success.

'If you're in between jobs, what's the great hurry to return to your *farm*?'

His voice oozed the kind of disdain people reserved for shameless freeloaders. But Faye didn't waste any effort on being affronted. She was used to being judged by her appearance. She stared back without answering. While he remained completely unaffected her silence.

'Perhaps you'd be better disposed to stay if I informed you that your work here *wouldn't* be voluntary?' His thin smile didn't take the sting out of his words. 'Casa di Fiorenti has a reputation for paying its employees well. Even its interns.'

He named a price that made her gasp. And immediately suspicious.

'Are you serious?' With just one month's pay she'd be able to secure her mother's room and board at New Paths for another year.

'That's for a mid-level employee. As Luigi's stepdaughter—'

'I don't want any handouts. Any job I undertake will be rewarded on merit, not because of my connection to Luigi,' she cut in, this time showing her affront.

His smile hardened. 'Believe me, you will work for it. I have no appetite for scroungers. What I intended to state was that as Luigi's stepdaughter you would be required to learn about the company from the ground up, as my parents required of me, preferably with a year at a cocoa-growing facility overseas. But, since you don't have that kind of time to spare, you'll stay here in Naples, where I can keep my eye on you.'

She flushed, the tension easing out of her even as he eyed her mockingly. 'Oh. I see.'

'The most appropriate place for you to start will be in the research and development department. I will reserve the right to rotate your position as I see fit.'

Faye wanted to protest at his assumption that she'd fall in line with his wishes. Or even stay in Italy. But as she glared at him for his high-handedness she knew she wouldn't walk away. Wouldn't squander the chance to make a significant impact.

Her mother's continued care and well-being would be assured at New Paths. And, as heartbreaking as it was to acknowledge it, her mother would probably not even register Faye's absence.

Pain twisted deep and she clutched the armrests tighter to hold it inside.

'No need to look so concerned, Faye. A hard day's work never killed anyone, as far as I know,' Maceo drawled, shattering her anguished thoughts.

She raised her chin. 'Save your insults, *signor*. I'm not afraid of hard work. As a matter of fact, you can put me to work immediately. The sooner I'm done here, the sooner we can be rid of each other.'

The triumphant gleam in his tawny eyes made the hairs on her nape quiver. And, after a beat, he once again helped himself to a scrutiny of her. A shiver flowed down from her neck, encompassing her body with a hot, electric awareness that left her peculiarly breathless.

'Curb your enthusiasm. I cannot, as you say, *put you to work*. Casa di Fiorenti has a professional reputation to safeguard. That includes a strict dress code in which you currently fall woefully short. And, as you weren't planning on being in Naples more than a day or two, I doubt you have the right attire to work anywhere besides your beloved farm,' he stated drily.

Her flush deepened but she refused to lower her gaze. While her taste in clothes was consciously individual, and she appreciated it didn't suit a corporate environment, she wasn't about to turn herself inside out to please this man.

'I'll accommodate your dress code...but only up to a point. I'm not changing who I am to suit anyone.' She gave herself an inner high-five when her voice emerged firm and strong.

His wry, twisted smile suggested he found her comment amusing. 'We're affiliated with several fashion houses. The HR department will ensure they're made available to you when you've filled out the appropriate forms.'

She tensed. 'What forms?'

Hooded eyes fixed more tightly on her. 'The usual employment forms. That will suffice.'

Faye forced herself to breathe out slowly. 'Is that necessary?'

Maceo's eyes narrowed. 'You must be aware how suspicious that sounds? How large *are* the skeletons in your closet, Miss Bishop?'

'How large are yours?' she threw back. 'You're the one insisting on this unnecessary assessment before you give me what's legally mine. I won't bare my life to you just so you feel better about doing whatever it is you're doing.'

He remained completely unfazed, leaning forward until the wide breadth of his shoulders filled her vision. 'You will give me your word that nothing in your background will embarrass me or my company.'

Ice engulfed her whole body, trapping her in her seat when all she wanted to do was jump up and flee those piercing eyes intent on digging beneath her skin. On baring the dark secrets she'd been forced to live with from birth.

'The only promise I'll make you is that I'm committed and hard-working. You have no right to make any other demands of me. Take it or leave it. But be warned: I won't simply disappear until you decide to honour Luigi and Carlotta's wishes.'

It was a wild bluff and she held her breath, hoping he wouldn't call her on it. He was the billionaire CEO of a staggeringly successful company, with all the clout and power that came with the position. She knew his legal team would chew her up and spit her out without so much as breaking a sweat should Maceo lift that haughty eyebrow to indicate they should do so.

Something hard and seasoned flickered in his gaze, making him appear much older than he was. As if he'd lived lifetimes and possessed harrowing tales to tell. Would those tales have anything to do with why he'd married Carlotta? Or explain that rabid mob of paparazzi downstairs?

Far from retreating from the frenzied curiosity eating her alive, Faye wanted to know more about this man. Wanted to unearth his every secret. Which was a dangerous state to inhabit when she had such deep, dark secrets of her own.

'I don't respond to threats, Miss Bishop,' he said, his words deceptively soft but effectively grounding her.

'I'm simply stating the truth, *signor*.'

'I've discovered "the truth" means different things to different people. I'm certain I'll find out *your* true mettle in the next six months.'

She gasped. '*Six months?* I can't... You can't force me to stay here that long.'

That eyebrow elevated, spelling out just how inconsequential he found her protest. 'I'm not forcing you to do anything,' he returned, far too smoothly. 'You're hardly my prisoner. Feel free to execute another dramatic exit, since you seem to specialise in those.'

'Three,' she blurted. 'I'll give you three months.'

'Four,' he countered immediately, his eyes gleaming with cut-throat anticipation. 'And I want your agreement that your connection to Luigi will only be divulged at my discretion.'

Four months of sacrifice in return for the ability to help thousands who needed it? With clever investment, the money from Luigi's bequest could stretch for years, perhaps decades. And, even while a large part of her remained horrified, and daunted by the thought of spending time under Maceo Fiorenti's laser eyes and dark suspicion, another part of her, emotionally centred on that bruising rejection all these years later, urged her to seize the opportunity.

Staying in Italy might reveal the truth once and for all—that Luigi had turned his back on her because of the stain of her birth that he hadn't been able to overlook. As much as it hurt to admit it, Matt had resurrected ghosts she needed to confront and, if not lay to rest, at least learn to cohabit with.

'Agreed. Four months and my…co-operation,' she accepted heavily.

His triumphant expression almost made her take it back. But he was already moving on. 'And at the end of it, you'll sell your share to me.'

'Or explore all my options and decide what's best for me.'

Burnished eyes held her in place. 'Selling it to me will be best, I assure you. No one else will give you the value I can.'

Why those words sent hot slivers of awareness through her, Faye refused to examine.

'Are we done here?' she asked, in a breathless rush she hoped he wouldn't notice.

Tawny eyes flickered, resting on her in a way that suggested he knew every thought racing through her head.

'One last thing. For the duration of your stay you'll reside at my villa in Capri. That way we won't have to have any tiresome debate about your room and board.'

The sensation of a silken net tightening around her made Faye shift in her seat. But there was no escaping his ferocious regard.

'No, thanks. I'll find my own accommodation.' Her heart sank at the thought of digging deeper into her meagre savings.

Keep your eyes on the prize...

'Did you see the paparazzi when you came in?' he asked, switching subjects.

Frowning, she nodded. 'Yes...'

'*Grande.* That is just a fraction of the press who follow me around on a daily basis. They'd love nothing better than to fixate on a shiny new object like you.'

Alarm dug into her belly. 'Why would they be interested in me?'

'Your arrival here isn't a secret. And you don't exactly blend into the background, do you, *arcobaleno*?'

Faye whizzed through the Italian words she knew, courtesy of that brief and idyllic time with Luigi before it had all turned to dust.

Arcobaleno. Rainbow.

Another more substantial sensation lanced through her. Heavier. Sinking low into her pelvis before setting off sparks in her private places. Sensations she'd smothered after that singular, soul-shredding experience with Matt.

'As far as I'm aware, that type of tabloid attention is reserved for notorious celebrities—so what does that make you?'

'I'm not here to indulge your curiosity, *arcobaleno*,' he replied with thick sardonicism. 'I'm simply giving you options. Take your chances at some cheap hotel with limited security or remain under my protection, where intrusion into your life will be minimal.'

'Why don't we spell out the real reason?' she asked. 'You really want me under your roof so you can keep an eye on me.'

'I will do so regardless of where you sleep, Faye, since I rarely take anyone at face value. It's entirely up to you whether you wish to sleep in comfort or in a hotel, with the constant inconvenience of the press hounding you and the unfortunate side effect of incurring my displeasure should you be tricked into speaking out of turn.'

A tiny scream gathered at the back of her throat. She swallowed it down because she knew in her bones that he'd love nothing better than to see her lose control. To have her confirm his every last preconception about her.

And Faye was sure that when she throttled back her irritation at his high-handedness she would see the benefit too. After all, he was saving her from unnecessary expense—money that could be put to better use elsewhere. But it still grated that she had to force herself to accept his strings-attached charity.

Her nails dug deeper into the armrests, but she froze when his mocking gaze dropped to her telling reaction. Forcing calm into her body, she replied, 'I'll stay at your villa. If you insist.'

He accepted her acquiescence with a simple nod, then reached for his phone. There was a short, rapid conversation in Italian, and then his eyes returned to her. 'My HR director is on her way. She'll get the ball rolling.'

The relief that attacked her midriff lasted all of two breaths before Faye registered that she was being dismissed—that Maceo was now engrossed in a document.

Insisting to herself that she was equally glad to be rid of him, she rose and willed her feet to turn about, dismissing him as easily as he'd dismissed her. She succeeded after several seconds, but it took every ounce of her willpower not to turn around and confirm that the feeling of his eyes boring into her back was nothing but her imagination.

Celebrating that tiny triumph felt essential. Because as she followed an impeccably dressed middle-aged woman out of the office, Faye's instincts screamed that she'd need every bit of ground she could retain when it came to Maceo Fiorenti.

Their battle was merely commencing.

CHAPTER THREE

THE MOMENT HER details were recorded on the system Maceo received an alert and accessed it. He despised himself for the unstoppable urge he couldn't deny. Far from being disillusioned after an hour spent grilling Faye Bishop, and having his suspicions confirmed that she was indeed only after the money from her share, he couldn't dismiss her from his mind.

He'd dissected her every quietly ferocious look, every word that had spilled from those Cupid's bow lips. He'd even pondered why she dressed the way she did. Why she inked flowers onto her skin. Why she had so little apprehension about irritating him, when everyone in his private and professional sphere went to unspeakable lengths do ensure the opposite. Even rattled, Faye gave as good as she got.

His gaze strayed to the chair she'd occupied, settling on the armrests she'd all but mauled in her bid not to sink those claws into him.

Maceo found his lips curving and immediately killed the action. The last hour changed nothing. All she'd done was spout words in an attempt to make him change his view of her. Anyone could claim hard work and commitment. The proof would reveal itself in the coming months.

Disgruntlement twisted in his gut. Before he'd met her, his intention had been for her to spend only three months at Casa di Fiorenti. So why had he pushed for six? And why the hell had he issued that directive that she stay at the villa?

While he'd been upfront about interest from the paparazzi, he hadn't divulged the fact that it was his own careful game, cultivated to keep them from digging into his family's past and discovering the unspeakable secret his parents and Luigi had moved mountains to hide. And, more than that, his own part in shortening the lives of his family.

Hindsight might be wonderful, but it was also cruel.

In raining judgement on his parents for harbouring the secret that had altered the very foundation of his beliefs, and shattered the pedestal on which they stood, he hadn't stopped to consider the consequence of his actions.

That he'd found out too late.

Now he had to live with the knowledge that his parents' carefully laid plans, their hopes and dreams for themselves and for him, had been destroyed because of *him*. Because of the implacable stance he'd taken when a cooler head and more flexibility might have saved him from this desolate path. The shame and guilt that rightly prevented him from contemplating any semblance of *famiglia*, or even a relationship for himself, were of his own making.

He had no one to blame but himself.

Grimly grounded by that reminder, he clicked open Faye's file.

His eyes narrowed, a tiny bolt of surprise charging through him as he perused her higher education history. She had a degree in sociology and business, achieved at the top of her class. And yet she chose to waste her time on a farm?

Beyond that there was nothing that should have prompted the tension she'd shown over filling in these forms. Yet it had been present.

Maceo paused when he reached her personal details, a hot wave curling though him as his gaze lingered on the marital status box she'd ticked: *none*.

None didn't mean *unattached*.

And it certainly didn't matter to him one way or the other.

He'd deprived his parents and Carlotta and Luigi of lifelong relationships, of decades of reaping the benefits of their hard work. Who was he to contemplate his own pleasure? A liaison? Or, heaven forbid, a *relationship*?

Jaw clenched, he dragged his gaze through the rest of the document.

Altogether, her history was unremarkable. And yet Faye Bishop was anything but… She was a deceptive little flame and she burned far hotter than her outward appearance implied. Was that why Carlotta had made him promise to test her before honouring her bequest? Because she'd experienced Faye's uniqueness for herself?

Basta!

He was spinning tales where there were none.

Rising, he strolled to his window, hoping for a

distraction. But not even the arresting view could replace a certain fairy-resembling creature with tiny claws, a sharp tongue…and a voluptuous body he couldn't quite erase from his memory banks.

But he hadn't battled the twin demons of guilt and shame on a daily basis without growing calluses. Summoning his iron will, he returned to his desk and for the next four hours successfully dismissed Faye Bishop from his thoughts.

An email from his lawyers confirming that Stefano and Francesco intended to contest their sister's will only roused in him amused anticipation. He'd hoped they would. Now he would ensure they walked away with nothing.

Maceo was contemplating his next move when the knock on his door came. His initial instinct to dismiss the unwanted visitor vanished when Faye Bishop's low, husky voice announced herself.

'Come.' His voice sounded thick, loaded with anticipation. Which irritated him endlessly.

Not enough to rescind his invitation, though.

He sat back and watched her enter, looking as colourful and unruffled as she'd been a few hours ago. *Dios*, she was even smiling—albeit at Bruno, his assistant, who smiled back before, catching Maceo's scowl, he hastily shut the door behind her.

The moment her gaze connected with Maceo's, her smile evaporated. He shifted again, his irritation increasing along with that pressure in his groin as she swayed in that ridiculous skirt towards him.

She stopped in front of his desk. He didn't invite her to sit.

'I'm done with HR,' she stated, after a moment of silence he didn't feel inclined to break.

'The experience wasn't too harrowing, I hope?'

She shrugged. 'It was what it was.'

Maceo just managed to stop himself from sneering. 'A nothing statement that couldn't be more useless if it tried,' he said.

She tilted her head, indigo eyes sparkling with amusement. 'You know, I thought it was just my presence that rubbed you the wrong way, but I'm starting to believe you're just naturally that way.'

A peculiar hollow opened up in his gut. 'And which way is that?'

'Hardwired to be bitter, cynical and just plain unpleasant.'

And guilty. How could he forget the guilt that ate him alive from the moment he woke till oblivion delivered him to his demons?

'I assure you I've never been *just plain* anything in my life.'

'Ah…so you're a special brand of acid rain, ruining the existence of anyone who happens to be caught within showering distance? When you were little, did you have an anti-hero cape, emblazoned with some unique dark lord logo?'

'There was never any need for such a garment. My extraordinariness sufficed. Still does.'

Her eyes widened and her delectable mouth gaped for a second before she caught herself. 'I shouldn't be surprised by that answer. And yet…'

'And yet you are? *Grande.* Know that I have the power and the wherewithal to pull this and any future rug from under you and we'll spare each other any surprises.'

Her amusement evaporated and Maceo felt another niggling sensation—this time disappointment. His exchanges with Carlotta had always been cordial, but spectres of the past and his demons had overshadowed their interactions. His banter with Faye was inconsequential, and yet he'd found himself savouring it the way he savoured the last mouthful of excellent espresso on his sun-drenched balcony before he faced the day.

'Your HR director said you wanted to see me. If it's just so we can hurl a few more insults at each other, then I'll pass. It's been a long day. I'd like to do something else that's not…*this.*'

She flicked her fingers between them in a manner supposed to indicate disdain, but Maceo spotted something in her eyes. Something that echoed his own disappointment.

He was fairly certain—not completely, since he didn't spare it more than a moment's thought—that it was the reason he powered down his computer and rose from his desk. And when he reached for his jacket and shrugged it on, he was aware her eyes followed his every move.

'Where are you staying?' he asked.

She frowned. 'Why?'

'Because you need to collect your things before we head for the villa. Unless you came to Italy with just the clothes on your back?'

Her headshake threatened the precarious knot of multicoloured hair atop her head. And seared him with the burning need to know how long her hair was.

'No. I have a case back at the hotel.'

She named it, and Maceo barely stopped himself from grimacing. It was little above a hostel—unworthy of the name *hotel*.

Si, relocating her to the villa was best. For one thing it would stop any awkward questions as to why Luigi's stepdaughter was staying in a hovel once the media got wind of who she was. He ignored the inner voice mocking him for hunting down further reasons for Faye to stay under his roof and headed for the door.

With clear reluctance she swayed towards him, then stopped. Her eyes locked on his. Blazed with an indigo defiance that tripped the blood rushing through his veins.

Maceo knew he should move from the doorway. Astonishingly, his feet refused to obey. For the first time this strange, intriguing creature was within touching distance, and he was wholly and irritatingly rapt with the need to do just that.

Touch. Explore. *Experience.*

This close, he became bracingly aware of her diminutive size. Faye barely came up to his shoulder. And yet her presence filled his senses, taunted him to take a deeper breath of air, to inhale her scent, imprint it on his very being.

Considering the vow he'd taken against experiencing any contentment or pleasure, Maceo knew he ought to feel guilt and shame. But the sensations rampaging through him were neither. This was a sort of...*electricity.*

Anticipation.

Arousal.

Had she been here, Maceo was certain Carlotta would have been amused. Perhaps for once she would not have stared at him with concern shadowing her eyes.

Because—

'Are we leaving any time soon?' Faye demanded, shattering his rumination.

But her bored tone belied the slight flaring of her nostrils and the budding awareness in her eyes that stated she wasn't immune to the charged atmosphere between them.

'After you,' he drawled, not so irritated that he didn't want to test the true mettle of her resistance. But only because it amused him. Nothing else. Certainly not because he wanted her closer. Wanted to decipher just what perfume she wore on her skin. The scent of her shampoo…

Like everything else in your life, she's a temporary fixture. Remember that.

She hesitated for a moment. Then she slipped into the gap he'd created, avoiding his eyes as she passed him and moved into his assistant's office.

Maceo's hand tightened on the door as he took a breath. Then another. Cherry blossom and fresh peaches. An ordinary combination. And yet on her it was a scent he wanted to chase to the source. Linger on and savour.

Dio mio, what was wrong with him? Not even at the age of eighteen, the last time he'd been remotely hormonal around the opposite sex, had his libido wreaked such havoc on his senses. Hell, even then he'd been cynical about the attention he'd received—had known that the power and prestige of his name had largely contributed to the zealous flattery that had come his way.

In the years since becoming CEO that theory had been repeatedly proved. Not even his being married had deterred women. He'd been propositioned on a regular basis. And all it had achieved was a lingering distaste in his mouth, reinforcing his decision that not seeking pleasure of any sort was the right path.

That fortifying goal had been a flaming signpost he'd followed. It had instilled in him a loyalty and fidelity to Carlotta that hadn't caused him a moment's wavering, despite the true situation of their marriage. But now, for the first time, Maceo had experienced a shift in that foundation. Followed by the realisation that he hadn't quite been able to drag his gaze from Faye's smooth skin or the feline movement of her body as she strode away from him.

Basta!

Curtly, he informed his assistant of his plan to work from his villa office and headed for the lift. He would relocate Faye, ensure she was under appropriate guard, and then forget she existed.

Thirty minutes later, he seriously feared his jaw would snap in two as her phone emitted yet another ping. She ignored it—again—seeming perfectly content to stare out of the window as they travelled to the heliport, her fingers curled around the handle of her small suitcase.

'Are you going to answer that?' he snapped, his gaze shifting to the large bag that held her phone somewhere in its shapeless depths.

'I will when I'm alone.'

Suspicion and intrigue built in him in equal measures, much to his annoyance. 'Don't hold back on my account. Surely any pertinent details I need to know, you've already apprised my HR department of?'

She studied him for a beat, then shrugged. 'Good, then it shouldn't bother you too much. Do we have far to go?' she added, stoking his annoyance further.

'We'll be at the helipad in less than five minutes.'

Her eyes widened. 'The heli— We're going to the villa by *helicopter*?'

Maceo was surprised…and, yes, intrigued…by the curbed delight in her voice. 'That's one of the modes of transport I prefer, *si*.'

'What's the other mode?'

'Speedboat.'

Her eyes grew rounder. Then she frowned. 'I've been on neither. Apologies in advance if anything untoward happens.'

Against his will, his lips twitched. 'Such as…?'

She shrugged again, drawing his eyes to the flowers dancing down one bare, shapely arm, to the delicate bones in her wrist. The tingling in his groin intensified. Grimly, he reeled himself in.

'I'm okay with heights…for the most part…but I don't know if I'll feel sick or not. Is that a thing on helicopters?'

'Motion sickness on helicopters is indeed a thing, *si*,' he rasped. Then watched her pert little nose wrinkle.

'Well, be warned, then. I guess seasickness is also a possibility. If I ever use your boat, that is.'

'I'll bear both in mind and keep the appropriate distance.'

'It's not too late to change your mind about inviting me to stay.'

Immediate rejection of that idea hardened in his gut. 'We will not rehash a matter that is already settled.'

'On your head be it,' she replied, in that tart little voice.

It promised barbs. Ones he felt peculiarly compelled to test, to stroke, to see how deeply they'd cut. It was a sensation that made him relieved to see they were approaching the helipad.

Relief morphed into intrigue when she alighted next to him and stared, stupefied, at the large aircraft that bore his family's logo.

'Good God, it's huge!'

Was it? He'd never given it a moment's thought. These days he occupied himself with safety rather than size, and he employed the best to ensure that no harm came to the things he cared about.

Up until a week ago it had been Carlotta. Now it was just Casa di Fiorenti. His own actions had ensured that.

The hollow ache expanded, the demons beginning to howl in glee.

You survived. Now you're alone. As you should be.

Exhaling around the tightness in his chest, he strove for calm. 'I suppose it is,' he drawled, once again disturbingly compelled by the emotions chasing across her face. 'Is that a problem?'

'Beyond making me think you're compensating for something with the size of your…equipment? Not at all.'

For the first time in a long time Maceo found

himself mildly astonished by a woman's forthright-
ness. The fact that it brought further acute attention to his manhood and a battering to the vow he'd
taken stunned him into stillness.

He clenched his jaw. Pleasure and companion-
ship weren't on the cards for him. And even if they
were it wouldn't be with this woman who stared
at him, her gaze daring, while the sunlight danced
in her rainbow hair and sparked her indigo eyes.

'Forgive me if I've broached a touchy subject.'

Maceo strode toward his aircraft. 'Don't insult
either of us. Your patently false tone neither begs
forgiveness nor concedes sensitivity. As for the slur
on my manhood—I don't feel the slightest inclination to prove you wrong.'

She arrived next to him just as a blush suffused
her face. The gaze that had held his so blatantly a
moment ago shifted away.

'A word of advice, *dolcezza*. Don't take on the
big dogs if you blush so easily. Trust me, I will out-
last you on any given day.'

With that, he held out his hand. After a tense
moment, she took it.

Maceo helped her into the helicopter and refused
to examine why he'd used his direct line to instruct his pilot to take extra care to make the journey smooth. Most likely because he wasn't in the
mood for further aggravation from her.

The moment they took off he busied himself answering emails and catching up on further business. Only to glance at her when she gasped.

'Is that the villa?' A sleek finger pointed in the general direction of Villa Serenita.

With a sigh, he slid his phone back into his pocket. '*Si.*'

'It's…breathtaking,' she whispered, her fingers braced against the glass as if caressing his home from afar.

He shifted in his seat. 'A genuine compliment?' he observed drily. 'I'm dumbfounded.'

She didn't respond. It was as if his residence had rendered her speechless.

He took the unexpected moment to see Villa Serenita through her eyes. The circumstances of his life thus far had impressed upon him the need not to take things for granted, the knowledge that one reality could be ripped from him to be replaced by another vastly less palatable but, if Maceo were honest, the place where he laid his head at night had stopped registering in the maelstrom of guilt and shame that had become his everyday life.

Now, as the chopper banked, he looked down at the villa his grandparents had built. The villa his parents had poured their hearts and souls into making a home while harbouring secrets that would shake its very foundation. The place where he himself had taken a stand that had destroyed everything.

'How old is it?' she asked.

Her tone conveyed genuine interest. 'It was a mere shell when my grandparents bought it, over seventy years ago, but the building is over two hundred years old. They kept to the original baroque style, but added their personal touch over the years.'

'And the pink?' she asked, tossing him a look before her gaze was drawn back down. 'Excuse my observation, but I didn't think it was a very... *manly* colour.'

Maceo shrugged. 'It's not a personal affront to my manhood, if that's what you're implying. In fact, I don't think any other colour will do the villa justice.'

To his surprise, she nodded. 'You're right. Now that I've seen it, I can't imagine it in any other shade but coral-pink.'

Was he truly discussing the effeminate colour of the building with this stranger? He gave a sharp shake of his head as the aircraft settled on the ground.

He threw his door open and stepped out, hoping the brisk air would restore some clarity. About to wave her in the direction of his staff and remove himself from her presence, Maceo once again found himself rooted in place. This time by the breathtaking smile on her face.

Had he missed something?

'I survived. Hurrah!' she gushed.

To his chagrin, she affectionately patted the side

of the helicopter. He watched the caress, his insides twisting with something close to disgruntled jealousy.

Si, definitely time for them to part company.

'*Bene*. I would have been most displeased had you decorated the interior of my aircraft with the contents of your stomach.'

'No worries there. I haven't had anything to eat since breakfast.'

He frowned. '*Che cosa?* Why not?'

'Because I was too busy answering several hundred questions for your HR manager.'

Before he'd fully registered his actions, he'd caught her elbow and strode with her from the helipad.

'Erm…where are we going?'

'To find you something to eat. Far be it from me to be tainted with a reputation for being inhospitable.'

He took the quickest way to the *salone* closest to his housekeeper's domain and tried to ignore his staff's shocked expressions when he strode into the kitchen.

Giulia, the elderly housekeeper who'd been part of the household since he was a boy, hurried towards him. '*Oh…buonasera, signor! Come posso aiutarla?*'

How could she help him? He stared down at Faye, realised he still held on to her. Registered too, that her skin was indeed smooth as satin, soft as silk. Warm. Supple. *Bellissima.*

'*Signor…?*'

Madre di Dio.

He snatched in a breath. 'Giulia, this is Faye Bishop. She'll be staying at the villa for the next few weeks. She requires a meal, and then would you show her to the Contessa Suite?'

Giulia was too seasoned to express the surprise reflected on his other staff's faces. The Contessa Suite had been his mother's, just along the corridor from Maceo's own, the Bismarck Suite.

But this too was a turn of events he didn't feel like dissecting.

As soon as Giulia had acknowledged his request, Maceo turned on his heel. He turned back just in time to see Faye gift one of her dimpled, breathtaking smiles to his housekeeper.

'I'm so sorry. I feel like I'm being foisted on you, Giulia…may I call you Giulia?'

He watched as Giulia melted beneath its brilliance before indulgently granting Faye leave to use her first name. Watched his visitor dump her bag on the floor before climbing onto the nearest island stool, leaning forward to rest her elbows on the counter, thereby displaying a larger swathe of creamy midriff.

'Whatever it is you're making, it smells amazing! I might have to beg you for the recipe.'

Aware that he was lingering and drawing more

peculiar looks from his staff, since they probably couldn't recall the last time he'd entered the kitchen, Maceo forced himself to keep moving. To banish the far too intriguing Faye Bishop from his mind.

Regardless of the novelty she presented for whomever she came into contact with—and he was beginning to think she'd spun whatever fairy magic it was that she practised around most people, including, unfortunately, Carlotta—*he* was Maceo Fiorenti. A vow of no entanglements in favour of the singular preservation of his family's legacy was his paramount objective. Nothing would sway him from that.

Not even an enchanting creature with the voice of a siren and skin plucked from his most erotic dream.

Maceo congratulated himself for blocking her out for several hours. Only when every last business detail had been attended to did he rise from his desk and stroll to his liquor cabinet. Drink in hand, he should be satisfied, and yet something niggled. A sense of elusiveness. Of loss…

His fingers tightened around the glass. *Si*, he missed Carlotta. He missed her laughter, especially during their occasional dinners, when he hadn't worked late into the night. He missed those moments when she'd so doggedly tried, and briefly succeeded, to pry him away from his demons. That was the reason he hadn't been able to use her favourite west-facing terrace since her death.

But that wasn't the source of his restlessness.

The puzzle unravelled itself in a flash of relief. Pico. Carlotta's eight-month-old cockapoo. Maceo hadn't seen him since he'd got home. While the dog had been unmistakably dejected in the days before and after Carlotta's death, he unerringly hunted Maceo down within minutes of his return home.

Except today.

Icy dread invaded his stomach. His merciless condemnation of his parents' and Luigi's actions had resulted in the very worst-case scenario, leaving him alone with only his demons for company. Surely the cosmos wouldn't be so cruel as to visit his transgressions on a defenceless dog in a bid to ensure he was truly alone in the world?

No...

Nothing had happened to Pico.

Not so soon after Carlotta.

Even he drew the line at the thought of such a turn of events.

Besides, the staff would have informed him if something untoward had happened.

Still, unable to shake the feeling, Maceo set his glass down. Exiting his office, he enquired after Pico from the first staff member he came across.

The young girl smiled. 'He was playing in the garden with Signorina Faye the last I saw him, *signor.*'

Certamente. Why had he assumed she wouldn't

commandeer yet another being the way she'd
wrapped his staff around her dainty little finger
within minutes of her arrival?

Realising his mood was slipping again, and that
his footsteps had drifted perilously close to the
extensive gardens in search of her, Maceo veered
about.

He'd had enough of Faye Bishop for today. Tomorrow would be soon enough to set out the precise parameters of her presence in his life. And
they certainly wouldn't include dragging things
that belonged to him under her spell—especially
the one creature that had kept him from feeling
completely unmoored.

CHAPTER FOUR

FAYE TURNED HER face up to the sun, taking a deep breath as warmth seeped into her bones. In this early witching hour, before the staff descended on the villa to begin ensuring it and the grounds remained in pristine condition, she liked to steal away and find a large rock near the private beach to watch the sunrise.

In the three weeks since her arrival she hadn't quite decided whether she loved the inside, with its stunning baroque architecture and soul-stirring paintings and masterpieces, or the outside, where a combination of tranquil gardens, awe-inspiring stone terraces and gorgeous landscaped grounds resided in beautiful juxtaposition with the churning sea beating itself relentlessly against the stone cliffs.

So far, she'd counted two dozen corridors and archways leading to intriguing courtyards, alcoves and neat little private gardens, each with its own unique mosaic or pedestal or fountain. Everywhere she turned she felt like a child, waiting to discover the next adventure.

In the first few days, when the staff had been open and forthcoming, she'd discovered that not only had Maceo's family lived here, Luigi and Carlotta had also made Villa Serenita their summer home, shortly after joining business forces with Maceo's parents, Rafael and Rosaria Fiorenti.

Faye wanted to dislike this place where Luigi had found happiness. Yet with each new discovery Villa Serenita worked its magic deeper into her soul.

But of course, there was the obligatory serpent within paradise.

Her thoughts reeled back to the morning after her arrival. Maceo had summoned her into his office at Casa di Fiorenti and laid down rules she'd apparently already flouted in the few hours she'd been under his roof.

First, she wasn't to distract the staff with unreasonable requests or overfriendliness. Second, she had free run of the villa but wasn't to grill the staff about its history or past residents. Third, and most importantly, Pico, the gorgeous puppy with chocolate eyes who'd stared at her so soulfully from his place on the kitchen floor that first evening, was off-limits. Never mind that the dog had taken to following her around wherever she went, stationing himself beside her seat at mealtimes, obedient, but irresistible enough to tempt small treats from her.

Faye had been perfectly content to flout that particular rule until Maceo had stopped her two days later, by simply keeping Pico in his private wing. Since then, her enquiries about Pico had met with guarded smiles from the staff.

It was clear Maceo was possessive about his dog. But Faye had weightier things on her mind. She was no further forward in discovering why Luigi had abandoned her so abruptly. Whether he'd believed he was doing her a favour by callously rejecting her and then, like Matt, pretending she was invisible. Matt had ignored her whenever he saw her on their university campus after she'd been foolish enough to reveal her secret.

The picture she'd found in the library a few nights ago, of a much younger Luigi and two other men, had thrown up even more questions.

One of the men was clearly Maceo's father; the resemblance was unmistakable. Equally striking was the third man's likeness to Luigi. But, while the unknown man was laughing in the photo, Luigi and Rafael remained serious. Borderline angry.

Rafael Fiorenti's expression was a familiar one she'd glimpsed on his son's face, but Luigi's expression was alien to her. Which drove home just how little she'd known her stepfather and her complete unawareness of the man named Pietro, according to the inscription on the back of the photo.

Who was Pietro? And why hadn't Luigi mentioned him in the two years he'd lived with her and her mother in Kent?

Because back then, every time you begged for stories of his homeland, he deftly changed the subject...

The ploy hadn't registered all those years ago, but it shuddered through her now. Pain gripped her again, threatening to settle inside her. Faye smothered it, dragging herself to the present. Namely, her meeting with Maceo this morning.

Initially it had been slated as a two-week evaluation, but Maceo had cancelled every meeting except today's. She remained on tenterhooks as to whether this meeting would go ahead but, judging from the butterflies buzzing in her stomach, Faye instinctively knew today was the day. So she couldn't afford to ponder the identities of mysterious strangers in photos.

With a sigh, she pulled her crimson sweater tighter over her pyjamas and made her way back through the garden. Letting herself into the villa by way of the large pantry and kitchen, she was met by the sight of Giulia, sliding a tray of pastries into the giant oven.

'*Buorngiorno, signorina. Signor* has asked for breakfast to be served early in the Salone Bianco. He wants you to join him.'

She froze in surprise. 'Really?' Maceo had yet to invite her to dine with him, either here in the villa or at work. In fact, he'd pointedly avoided her in both places.

Giulia nodded. '*Si.* He wishes to have breakfast in half an hour.'

So the third degree was starting at the breakfast table?

She summoned a smile for Giulia and hurried to her room. She whizzed through her shower on automatic, only forcing herself to concentrate when she walked into the dressing room that was three times the size of her Devon bedsit.

Three weeks on, Faye still couldn't quite believe her suite's opulence or size. Even more unbelievable was the personal wardrobe that had arrived by the boxful the morning after her arrival. When the HR director had informed her she was entitled to a new wardrobe as part of joining Casa di Fiorenti, Faye had expected to be handed a small allowance and pointed in the direction of the nearest high street boutique. Instead, what seemed like the contents of entire haute couture showrooms had arrived at the villa via speedboat. She'd chosen the designer who most suited her taste and returned the rest.

Now, she selected a deep lilac knee-length dress, a fuchsia belt she'd embellished with embroidered flowers, and added the matching brooch handmade by her mother. The pops of colour eased her nerves, but her insides still quaked slightly as she stepped into her shoes, grabbed her bag and left the suite.

The Salone Bianco lived up to its name in sun-splashed resplendence. The only thing that *didn't* gleam white was the gold marble edging the walls of the octagon-shaped room. Every piece of furniture was white, including the lavish dining table, at the head of which sat Maceo, his head buried between the pages of an Italian newspaper.

He didn't remain that way for long.

Faye's throat dried as he slowly lowered the

paper and speared her with dark tawny eyes. '*Buorngiorno.* I'm glad you could join me,' he drawled, his voice low, deep and maddeningly invasive to her senses.

She'd only caught brief glimpses of him in the past three weeks, and for the life of her she couldn't drag her gaze from the play of sunlight on his hair, and his broad shoulders and impressive biceps, to which his pristine shirt eagerly clung.

Several superlatives jumped into her brain, but the only one appropriate enough—the only one that effortlessly fitted him, as if coined especially for him—was *magnificent.* He was wasted, merely sitting at a breakfast table when he could've graced the cover of Italian *Vogue* or *GQ* or some other plush magazine strictly dedicated to cataloguing unique male beauty.

If you were into that sort of thing.

Which she wasn't.

So why was her breathing jagged? Her insides going into free fall with each second she spent staring at him? Why, amongst all the adverse emotions cascading through her, was there…*anticipation*?

The sensation irritated her enough to make her reply crisp. 'Was it an invitation? It sounded remarkably like a summons.'

His gaze swept leisurely down over her dress. It lingered at her hips before returning to her face. Faye couldn't quite read the look in his eyes, but whatever lurked there made her blood run hotter.

'If pretending will stop either of us from getting indigestion, then by all means I'll play along. Thank you for accepting my invitation to breakfast. Please sit down, Faye,' he said.

Her breath caught in her throat. The sound of her name on his lips still evoked such sensuality she wanted to request…no, *demand* he say it again.

And what was that if not utter madness? Hadn't she learnt her lesson with Matt, the one time she'd dropped her guard enough to contemplate an experience resembling normality, only to be ruthlessly reminded that she was *nothing* like normal? That she was an abomination?

The reminder dredged up pain, but it also grounded her enough to ignore the cocked eyebrow that was telling her she risked humiliating herself by her deer-caught-in-the-headlights stasis. With stilted movements, she pulled out a chair and sat down.

'Coffee?' he offered smoothly.

'Tea, please. Thank you,' she tagged on, determined to wrestle some civility into this meeting.

A butler glided forward, poured her tea and then, after offering a platter of fruit and an assortment of breakfast meats, melted away.

Silence throbbed between them. Maceo was seemingly content to devour one cup of espresso after another while perusing his paper. At last, with perfect timing, just before she gave in to the urge to fill the silence, he spoke.

'You've spent a few weeks now at Casa di Fiorenti. What's your verdict? Do you still consider it the very heartbeat of the monster that deprived you of your stepfather or have you revised your opinion?' His voice dripped cynicism.

Despite the unfair assessment, she found herself flushing, because there was a kernel of truth in his words. Luigi had been in her life for only two years, but they'd been formative years that had given her a glimpse of what a family could be like. Maybe she would have got over his leaving them if she hadn't been confronted with Casa di Fiorenti confectionery and the memory of his desertion with every supermarket she'd walked into. That ever-present evidence had done nothing to heal the hurt of her loss, but she'd tried to cope with it. Until Matt.

She tried for a diplomatic answer not steeped in anguish. 'I never considered it monstrous. I just—'

'Wanted so very much to dislike it?'

She shrugged, sipped her tea to delay answering. 'Maybe.'

'And now?'

She couldn't hold back the truth. 'So far as I can tell…it's not so bad.'

'Damned with faint praise,' he said drily. 'Tell me what you really think, Faye.'

Again her name on his lips sent a frisson down her belly, and then shamelessly between her thighs. 'Why? What does it matter?'

He didn't answer for a long spell, drawing her attention to his face in a vain attempt to see behind his enigmatic façade. 'Because I made a promise.'

The answer was unexpected enough to widen her eyes. 'You did?'

He gave a brusque nod. *'Si.'*

'To who?' she demanded, her heart beating for a different reason.

'Who do you think?'

'Your...your wife?' Why did that word continue to lodge a dart of unease inside her? What did it matter to her one way or the other that he'd been married?

Because thinking of him belonging to someone else unsettles you.

And not because of Carlotta's connection to Luigi.

He shrugged. 'For some reason she seemed to want you to form a good impression of the things she cared about.'

That surprised Faye. 'She said that?'

His eyes speared into hers before they flicked away. 'She said many things. I'm yet to conclude if they were the result of facing her own mortality or what she truly believed.'

She gasped. 'How can you say that? Who are you to decide?'

'If not someone in a unique position to sort fact from fiction without the inconvenience of frothy emotion, then who?' he bit out.

'And you would dishonour her by discarding her wishes as you please?'

His face hardened, his eyes growing flat and hard. 'She trusted me to do the right thing because she knew I wouldn't be swayed by…what do you English call it?…*flights of fancy*. And that trust is what I will honour.'

She bit her lip to stop another hot, condemning retort from slipping out. She even tried to eat, despite her throat threatening to clog. After a few bits of toast and scrambled egg, she set her cutlery down. 'If you want me to form a good impression then why instruct your staff to stop talking to me?'

Faye wasn't aware of quite how much his edict had hurt until she blurted the question. He froze, his eyes turning that unique tawny shade and filling with an icy fury that sent shivers down her spine.

'Because there's gossip and there are facts.'

'Do you trust your own staff so little?'

Again he shrugged. 'Carlotta was beloved by everyone, and they're in mourning. I didn't want you to be swayed by superfluous emotion.'

'And you? Aren't you in mourning?'

His face closed up. 'My emotions are none of your concern.'

'Are you sure? I think your emotions directly affect our interaction. You can't seem to look at me or speak to me without attaching unsavoury labels. Which is curious, because I've discovered a few things about you, *signor.*'

'Have you?' His tone was bored in the extreme.

'For someone who demands propriety from others, you certainly like notoriety. Some would even think you've gone out of your way to court it.'

Faye could've sworn he stiffened at her remark; that something resembling wariness twitched in his face. But he shrugged. 'My relationship with the paparazzi is—'

'None of my concern?' she finished, smiling mockingly.

'Exactly so. Carlotta found baiting the media amusing. So I indulged her.'

'Why?' From what she'd read about Carlotta, the woman had been the epitome of class and poise. Faye struggled to picture her dallying with the tabloid press.

'Because it was either let them continue to print hurtful things about her or control the narrative by giving them something specific to print,' Maceo replied, then looked almost bewildered by the truth he'd divulged.

'So it was all a game to you?'

'Isn't life one form of game or another?' he queried cynically, but she saw the muscle ticking in his jaw, his fingers tightening on his cup.

There was more to this than merely taunting the press for laughs.

The picture she'd discovered in the library, now

tucked into a book on her bedside table, rose to her mind. But instinct warned her now wasn't the time to ask about it.

Faye shook her head, her insides tightening with bitterness, sadness and shame. 'Not to me. To me life is very real and very serious, *signor*.'

His gaze rose to linger on her hair, then the bright spots on her attire. 'And yet your outward appearance implies otherwise.'

'Don't judge me because I prefer not to dwell in sombreness, like you.'

To her utter surprise, he smiled. It didn't reach his eyes, of course, but the startling radiance of it was enough to make her forget to breathe. When she did suck in a breath, his gaze fell to her breasts.

A different sort of atmosphere charged the air. Like the start of a firework display in the far-off distance, growing closer, more seismic, by the second.

It was the same sensation that had permeated their interaction in his office three weeks ago. One steeped in sexual awareness that still made her hot and restless and twisty inside, especially at night, long after she'd gone to bed, curiously fighting sleep until she heard the distinct sound of his helicopter landing.

That maddening awareness had driven her to her bedroom's arched windows once, to catch a glimpse of him. She'd regretted it deeply when Maceo had caught her in the act, halting mid-stride as he crossed the lawn. For an eternity he'd stared up at her, paralysing her in place with those piercing eyes, before icily dismissing her and sauntering into the villa.

'I don't hear your denial that this is all camouflage for what you're really like underneath the... gaiety.'

Faye was glad she'd set her cutlery down because she'd have dropped it and given herself away as a mini earthquake moved through her. As it was, she took the altogether cowardly option of not meeting his gaze, unnecessarily straightening her napkin as she willed her panicked heartbeat to slow.

Because the truth was, she *was* hiding. Covering up the dark stain of her existence. Tuning out the dark, menacing voice that declared her circumstances would never be normal. That the formation of intimate bonds, physical or emotional, while carrying the burden she did was impossible.

Matt had proved that with his raw and callous rejection.

'Once again we seem to have avoided the subject at hand. Or did you really invite me to breakfast to discuss my wardrobe?'

He stared at her for a beat longer, then sat back. 'I'm meeting with my R&D department today to discuss your evaluation. This is a chance for you to warn me of any...irregularities.'

Returning to firmer ground, she smiled. Learning how Casa di Fiorenti went about selecting new flavours for their exclusive brand had been enlightening. And unexpectedly thrilling. 'Thanks for the heads-up, but I'm not worried in the least about my performance.'

'*Bene*. I hope that "performance" holds up under more rigorous scrutiny next Saturday.'

'What's happening then?'

'Casa di Fiorenti holds a pre-summer party for its top executives and their families, and its business partners. Two hundred people will spend the afternoon here at the villa. You will be required to attend.'

'But… I'm not an executive.'

'No, you're not. But while I'm perfectly happy for you not to attend, it was one of Carlotta's wishes for you see the *famiglia* side of the company. The party is a tradition she started. We haven't missed one in twenty years.' There was a definite bite in his tone when he used the Italian word, but again his face was devoid of emotion.

'Why did she want me there?' Faye asked, something tugging in her chest.

'I can't answer for her. But you will attend. And while you're there you will ensure nothing you do or say brings the company into disrepute.'

Faye bristled. 'Am I allowed to even speak at all, or shall I pretend to be mute?'

'We agreed that revealing yourself as Luigi's stepdaughter will be at my discretion. I'm simply reminding you to weigh the options and be prepared to deal with the outcome should you decide to out yourself.'

She couldn't help but wonder if this was another test. A way to discover whether she was worthy of the gift Luigi and Carlotta had bestowed on her from beyond the grave. But, again, while she'd have loved to throw his invitation in his face, attending this party might deliver the answers she sought.

'I'll be there. And I'll do my best not to disgrace the family name.'

For the briefest second his fists balled. Then eased. 'That's all I ask,' he replied mockingly.

He rose, caught up the bespoke jacket draped over a nearby chair and shrugged into it. The act of watching him don his jacket held her immobile, heat swirling in her belly.

'Are you coming?' he drawled, staring down at her.

'What?'

He glanced pointedly at his watch. 'Your evaluation is scheduled for eight a.m. Do you plan on being there?'

'I… Of course.'

He stepped close to her chair and Faye scrambled up, unwilling to be disadvantaged by Maceo towering over her. Flustered, she nudged her chair back with a little too much force and stumbled.

The sequence of events was swift and dizzying. With lightning reflexes Maceo caught the toppling chair with one hand and her waist with the other as she tottered on her heels. Then, in direct contrast to the preceding moment, the world stilled.

Faye wanted to ignore the sizzling intensity of the hand holding her, the thawing of his cool tawny regard, the heat fluttering in her chest and the flood of hot awareness through her veins.

She could do none of the above.

Without uttering a word Maceo Fiorenti commanded her body, her speech, the very air she breathed. Or the air she *couldn't* breathe because he'd commandeered that too.

Fierce eyes stared down at her, as if he was trying to see beneath her skin. Had his hand just tightened on her? Had he drawn her closer? Or was it all in her fevered imagination?

As a child, she'd foolishly stuck her finger into an electric socket. That was nothing compared to the sensation coursing through her now as Maceo tugged her closer. The look in his eyes was no longer indifferent. Or dismissive. His eyes smouldered with a definite fire. One that promised consumption. *Annihilation.*

And, far from shying away from it, denying the sort of danger that could destroy her, for a suspended moment in time Faye yearned to embrace it. To *feel* that electric shock. Experience that burn.

That insanity was the reason she raised her hand with a compulsion she couldn't deny, caressed the swathe of skin just above his collar where a vein pulsed, then brushed her fingers against the chiselled perfection of his jaw to the thin but character-ful scar halfway between his chin and his mouth. She lingered, explored, while her heart banged hard against her ribs and electricity consumed her from temple to toes.

Maceo inhaled sharply, his gaze dropping to her mouth before darting back to her eyes, his look of hunger so intense she gasped.

The sound forked between them, alive and de-manding.

With an Italian curse steeped in gruff de-nial, Maceo stepped back. His gaze turned from shocked to censorious as he dropped his hands. *'Per al amor—'*

He cut off his own words and whirled away from her.

'I… I'm sorry. I didn't mean—' It was her turn to curb her words. Because she had meant to touch him.

'I'm not sure what you think you're playing at, Miss Bishop, but I'd caution you against trifling with me. Under any circumstance.'

His voice was a hundred blades, slashing her to shreds. Death by a thousand warnings when one would have sufficed.

'Just so we're clear, I don't mix my business with pleasure. *Ever.*'

That final word was icily bitter. She gripped the edge of the table to steady herself against curiously searing disappointment. 'But I'm not your business, am I? I'm Luigi's. Carlotta's by extension. To you, I'm a temporary burden, thrust upon you. You could be rid of me immediately, but are choosing not to. Which begs the question: which one of us is the glutton for punishment in this scenario?'

'I have never taken the easy way out in anything, and nor do I intend—much as it'll give us both satisfaction. As for your little…indulgence just now, you will ensure it doesn't happen again.'

But Faye knew it hadn't been all her. She'd seen the hunger in his eyes. Felt the pressure in his touch. His very male reaction against her hip.

'Then do me a favour. Next time let me fall.'

He looked momentarily confused. *'Che cosa?'*

'You stopped me from falling just now. Next time, if you're not certain you won't blow things out of proportion, keep walking.'

He seemed stunned by her response. Faye was certain no one had dared speak to the great Maceo Fiorenti that way in his life.

He took his time sliding the single jacket button into its hole, for all the world completely unaffected by the turbulent little incident. Back under rigid control, he inclined his regal head towards the door. 'I will bear that in mind. Shall we?'

The journey to the jetty where his speedboat waited to ferry them to the office was conducted in tight silence. One Faye used to wrestle her senses back under control. By the time she stepped aboard and hurried to the farthest plush seat, she could draw half a breath without fruitlessly chasing Maceo's scent of citrusy aftershave and disgruntled man. She could even avoid glancing his way for several seconds at a time. Pretend his tall, imposing body *wasn't* continuing to wreak havoc on her senses.

She breathed a sigh of dubious relief when they entered Casa di Fiorenti twenty minutes later and he was immediately set upon by his assistant. But even as she scurried away she knew the reprieve wouldn't last. Nevertheless, she locked herself away in the restroom, under the guise of fixing her slightly windblown hair, desperately attempting not to relive those moments in the dining room, as she needlessly straightened her clothes and prepared herself for the grilling to come.

Sure enough, the moment she sat down in the same conference room where she'd first met him, Maceo proceeded to dissect everything she'd learned in the past three weeks. When the head of the department repeatedly assured him that she was in no way slacking in her duties, Maceo turned those tawny eyes on her.

'Tell me the most important thing you've learned so far, Miss Bishop,' he tossed at her.

They were back to *Miss Bishop*, were they? Why did that send a dart of hurt through her?

'I can't speak for all departments, of course, but Signor Triento is an excellent leader. He trusts his staff to deliver on their goals without being a tyrant about it. I'm especially pleased with my assignment to help come up with new flavours for a limited-edition Christmas collection. I already have a few ideas.'

Alberto Triento beamed at her, before a glare from his boss swiped the smile away.

'I wasn't aware we were giving interns such leeway,' Maceo groused, his eyes narrowing on Alberto.

The older man shrugged. 'There is nothing wrong with testing new talent. It might come to nothing. Or it might bear fruit. We won't know until we explore, *si*?'

He invited agreement, but Maceo's gaze grew colder before, as if he'd grown bored of throwing his weight around, he dismissed Alberto.

Faye knew better than to assume he was done with her too. 'So, did I pass muster?'

'Try not to get carried away with the novelty of it all. And bear in mind we test hundreds of flavours every year. Very few make the cut into production.'

'But I get to eat chocolate as part of my job. I'm failing to see the downside to that!'

He pursed his lips, as if her observation had irritated him.

'Why the R&D department?' Faye asked in the silence that followed.

He paused a beat before answering. 'That was Luigi's department. It became Carlotta's after his death. She was an effective marketing director, but

Luigi won her over to his side and she grew to love discovering new products.'

Grateful for that morsel of information, Faye felt a lump rise in her throat. 'Thanks for telling me. It sounds like they had a lot in common?'

Eyes that saw far too much rested on her. 'You really knew so little about your own stepfather?'

It sounded like an accusation. But she was still a little too wrung out after that breakfast incident to indulge in another skirmish.

She shrugged. 'We lost touch when he returned to Italy.'

The gleam in his eyes said he wasn't buying it. 'Italy is hardly the other side of the world. How old were you when he left? Thirteen? Fourteen?'

'Eleven.'

Some people experienced life-changing events that lasted a moment. She'd experienced two years that had given her a glimpse of what a true family looked like. Luigi's complete silence after leaving her and her mother had thrown everything into question—including her own worthiness. Learning of her mother's harrowing secret and her own genesis had thrown up further questions.

It had been a burden she'd resigned herself to living with.

Until Matt's declaration.

Until Carlotta's persistence had opened the box she'd strived to keep shut.

As much as Faye despised the need to confront

her emotional wounds, she knew it was part of the arduous process towards gaining a semblance of sanity, including exorcising the ghosts of Luigi's desertion.

She took a deep breath. 'He turned his back on me when I was a *child*. So why should I have made any moves?'

Dark shadows flicked over Maceo's face. 'Perhaps he had his reasons?'

Pain seared deeper. 'Everyone has their reasons. Perhaps he should've been man enough to explain his to me instead of—'

'Instead of…?' Maceo coaxed icily.

'Doesn't matter now.'

'I beg to differ. You seem overly…emotional.'

'And you pride yourself on having no emotions at all. So why do you keep pushing me?'

'Contrary to your belief, I care about Luigi and Carlotta's memories. I push you as a warning to you not to consider soiling them.'

'You care so much about Luigi that you married his wife?' she blurted, before she could stop herself. Then knew immediately she'd gone too far.

He grew statue-still, perfectly emulating the marble masterpieces that littered his homeland. 'Don't stray into territory you don't understand.'

What was there to understand? And why couldn't she leave it alone?

'Enlighten me, then. Surely I'm not the first person to wonder at your…*interesting* match.'

He surged upright, and despite his calm breathing his eyes blazed volcanic fire. 'This meeting is over. You may leave.'

She took her time to gather her papers, stand and face him across the conference table. 'Of course, *signor*. But before you accuse me of prying, remember I'm trying to find out about my stepfather. And you factor into that. So tell me what I want to know. Or don't. But I'm not leaving Italy until I have a few answers of my own.'

Including to that mysterious picture someone had hidden between the pages of an obscure book.

Faye Bishop was well and truly underneath his skin.

Distancing himself from her, as he'd done these past three weeks, had simply thrown up more questions. More intrigue. He'd hoped the evaluation meeting might provide clarity. Or, if he was being completely truthful, expose glaring flaws that would justify his assumptions about her.

Alberto Triento's fawning over his newest employee proved there would be no help from that source.

As to what had nearly happened at his breakfast table… That unbridled heat…that *hunger* he'd never experienced before… That continued insistent tingling in his very being…

Her fingers had been on his face, on that scar no other human had dared to touch, the scar that served as a daily reminder of what he'd done…

Maceo shoved a hand through his hair and resisted the supremely uncharacteristic urge to fidget. Which was laughable. Except laughing was the very last thing he felt like doing.

No, what he found himself reverting back to, with uncanny and alarming frequency, was wondering what she would have tasted like had he succumbed to that fevered urge and kissed her...

He sat down, resisting the urge to rise again.

He was Maceo Fiorenti. He didn't fidget and he didn't pace. The vow he'd taken in that hospital bed to deny himself of everything he'd robbed his parents of had held true for the last decade. So why was he being tested now?

I'm not sure what your game is, Carlotta. She's insolent, ungrateful and far too colourful to be taken seriously. Not to mention nosy to the point of rudeness.

Then why are you here?

Maceo heard her amused voice so distinctly he wouldn't have been at all surprised to find Carlotta right beside him on this marble bench set before the family mausoleum, with her signature bright smile and that perfectly plucked eyebrow arched in sweet mockery.

The fresh flowers he'd instructed to be delivered gave off their sweet scent even while reminding him that the scent of cherry blossom was sweeter to him these days. Ever since he'd caught a certain woman's scent and been unable to divorce himself from it.

That scent had filled every corner of his being at his breakfast table, when he'd almost lost his mind. Almost, but not quite. He'd stepped back from the brink of that insanity.

Shame, Carlotta's distinctive voice mused.

Maceo glared harder at the memorial in front of him. 'I should finish this now,' he said aloud. 'Today. Hand over the inheritance and the letter and be done with it, no?'

Silence greeted his question. He grimaced, knowing he wouldn't take the easy route. He'd made a vow to the woman who'd put her own grief on hold in order to help him secure his legacy. Without his word, what was he?

The reminder he carried with him everywhere burned against his breastbone. With not quite steady hands he reached into his pocket and pulled out the piece of paper, despite the fact that every line was seared in his memory.

It was a replica of the framed one he'd discovered amongst his parents' belongings and now kept in his bedside drawer. A joint lifelong 'to do' list, scribbled on a cheap restaurant napkin, back when his parents had been engaged. Maceo ran his gaze down the list, his chest tightening at the last abrupt tick. The vice intensified as he forced himself to read through every item his parents hadn't been around to tick off.

Because of him.

He'd deprived them of it. It was only right he stuck to *his* vow of deprivation.

Returning the note to his pocket, he stared at Carlotta's plaque.

'She's prying where she shouldn't be,' he said aloud.

Then do something about it.

The words seeped into his bones with a simplicity that stunned him. Rather than keep his distance, he needed to keep a closer eye on Faye. He might despise secrets, but allowing her to pry, to risk airing his family's dirty laundry wasn't an option.

He brushed his fingers over Carlotta's name, his stomach churning with guilt and shame as he flicked his gaze over his parents' memorial.

You should be here. Or I with you.

He bunched his fists, fighting the ever-present battle not to be drawn into that dark hole. He had a duty to perform. And when it was over...when nothing stood between him and the chasm...what then?

He veered away from the question and his monumental guilt and headed for his Alfa Romeo, parked behind him in the private cemetery.

'What do you mean, she's gone *clubbing*?'

The very word tasted wrong on his lips, and he wasn't surprised when his assistant shot him an apprehensive look.

'I believe it's someone's birthday in her department. According to the email, they're going to dinner and drinks, clubbing afterwards.'

Maceo had no valid reason for the haze that passed over his eyes. Or the sharp sting of disappointment that trailed behind it. Perhaps it was because for the first time in recent memory he'd put work to one side. He'd been prepared to subject himself to dinner with Faye, perhaps even answer a few of her questions. Only to find she'd made plans that didn't involve him.

He snarled at the snide inner voice. He had a *right* to be disgruntled. He was her boss.

'Have my car brought around and alert my pilot. I'm leaving.'

'Si, signor.'

To his credit, Bruno didn't express surprise at Maceo's uncustomary early exit from the office. He jumped into action, leaving Maceo simmering in unsettling temper.

He was still seething after a solitary dinner, an unremarkable stroll through the gardens with a very solemn Pico and his first nightcap. He refused to glance at his watch, although the opulent antique clock in his study did an adequate job of telling him it was close to midnight.

The sound of a water taxi propelled him to the French doors. From that vantage point he watched Faye step onto the jetty with a grace and agility that wouldn't have been remiss in a ballet dancer. She turned towards the driver as he handed her something. It took a moment—and a peculiar tightening in his gut—to realise it was her shoes.

She laughed in response to the driver's words, one hand lifted to tuck back a swathe of lilac hair in the fluttering breeze, the other clinging to her shoes. The carefree spectacle, for some absurd reason, tripped his irritation into fury.

He made the journey from study to jetty without recalling having moved.

Extracting his wallet, he shoved a handful of notes at the driver and barely heard the man's effusive thanks.

'Did you have a good time?' he asked Faye, aware of the ice dripping from his voice. And not caring one little bit.

CHAPTER FIVE

SHE WHIRLED AROUND and the smile slowly drained from her face.

This day of firsts continued to pummel him. Because, absurdly, Maceo felt a dart of regret that she was no longer smiling.

'Yes, I did,' she murmured. 'And before you give me a hard time—'

He waved her away. 'You don't need my permission to come and go as you please.'

Wry astonishment flared in her eyes. 'I beg your pardon, but have you tried telling that to your face?'

A smile tugged at his lips, despite the irritation bubbling in his veins. Staring past her to the disappearing water taxi achieved the desired effect of restoring his disgruntlement. 'A heads-up would have been nice.'

Her lips pursed. 'So you could give me a hard time about it before I left?'

'So I could've cancelled the plans I made for dinner.'

Her eyes widened in shock. Maceo chose not to be insulted.

'I… You wanted to take me out to dinner?'

'Not out in public, no. I thought we could have dinner together here at the villa.'

Her long lashes swept down. 'Oh. Well, since you've been treating me like an unwanted guest for the last three weeks, dining with you was the last thing I expected.'

He frowned. 'You exaggerate. I've treated you in no such way. And I have it on good authority that your every wish has been catered for.'

Because he'd instructed it to be so. He had affluence to spare, after all, and at the end of this he wanted her amenable to selling that share to him.

Is that all you want?

He ignored the question as she sighed. 'I'm not about to get into another argument with you, Maceo. Or, heaven forbid, offer my views on the way you host guests in your home.'

A rush of heat through his veins stilled him for a moment. And then he brutally dismissed it. There should be nothing *pleasing* about her using his name. She'd invited him to use hers, after all. Yet he yearned to hear her say it again. Perhaps even moan it when he explored that lush lower lip of her with his fingers? His lips?

Dio Santo, what was wrong with him?

His hand went to his breastbone, blindly seeking the list. The *reminder*. But it was still in his jacket, discarded in his study. Much as he was discarding his vow—

No. Never that.

He dropped his hand as she walked past him and headed for the house. Again he felt that maddening compulsion to follow, to let his gaze wander over her, take in those long, supple legs and slim, delicate ankles.

'Was there a particular reason for this dinner?' she threw at him over her shoulder.

For an unguarded moment he wanted to toss back a petty retort that if she'd wanted to find out she should've let him know her plans. Thankfully, the moment passed.

'I was struck by a sudden generosity and decided to answer a few of your questions over a good meal.'

She'd started to climb the steps leading to the terrace, but she stopped and pivoted, her movements entrancingly graceful. 'You were going to tell me about Luigi?'

Her eyes glowed in the dark, luminous and expectant. Torrid heat built within him, flaring until it engulfed his whole body.

'Perhaps. I hadn't quite made up my mind.'

She tilted her head, indigo eyes narrowing. 'Do you take pleasure in toying with me, Maceo?'

The very thought of trifling with her sent a heavy pulse of arousal through him. *Dio*, he either needed to find a different sort of entertainment or to have his head examined.

'You missed your chance to find out.'

Sumptuous lips pressed together. 'How do I even know this dinner plan you claim to have had is the truth? Maybe you're trying to make me feel bad about something that didn't exist.'

'Do you feel bad about *anything*?'

She stiffened. 'What?'

He summoned righteous outrage, hoping it would erode this…this *lust* that insisted on confusing him. 'You had a chance to get your answers from Carlotta and you denied her. Do you feel bad about that?'

She simply stared at him. Bold and seeking. And for the first time in his life Maceo felt the strangest inclination to back down. Look away.

'What happened to you…?' she murmured eventually.

Ice cracked his spine. 'What?'

The light in her eyes dimmed. 'Never mind. I'm wasting my breath.' She started to walk away.

Without stopping to consider the wisdom of it, he reached out and captured her elbow. 'Clearly you have something on your mind. Let's hear it,' he invited silkily. 'A nightcap, perhaps? Maybe that will make you more civil?'

Her eyes shadowed, then dropped away. 'I don't drink. Never have.'

'Any particular reason why not?' he asked.

'Because a clear head is important to me.'

'What a peculiar answer.'

She shrugged. 'You find me peculiar already. What's one more thing?' She pulled away, and with searing reluctance Maceo let her go.

In the *salone*, he strode over to the drinks cabinet, poured mineral water with a dash of lime and held it out to her. She took it, but made no move to drink.

'So, is clubbing your ideal sort of entertainment?' he asked, feeling his reluctance to be done with her eating deeper into him.

'I can take it or leave it.'

'And the R&D team? Can you take or leave them too?'

'What *is* this, Maceo? You've gone from warning me against even breathing in your presence to outright socialising with me?'

Maceo ignored her scepticism. If he was to get her onside to claim that share, he needed to tread carefully. 'Ask me what you want to know about Luigi,' he invited, giving up on making small talk he didn't care about.

The glass trembled in her hand. She tightened her fingers, lowered her head. 'Did…did he ever mention me?'

Maceo shook his head. 'I didn't know you existed until a few weeks ago.' The revelation still grated—badly. *So many secrets...*

Hurt darted across her face and he watched her slowly stroll over to the sofa. She sat down, looking a little lost as she stared into her glass.

'I suppose that means he never mentioned my mother either?' she asked.

Despite her efforts to conceal it, he heard wariness in her tone, saw the way she avoided his gaze.

His hackles rose. 'No, he didn't. Neither did my parents.'

Certainly they had never told him the full story. A story with layers he might never uncover now everyone involved had perished.

He couldn't keep the bitterness from merging with the guilt that churned through his stomach. He'd pushed for transparency and all he'd been left with were ashes and a life of desolation. Because how could he dare to grasp for anything resembling contentment when he'd deprived his own parents of theirs? When each time he looked in the mirror he experienced the guilt of being alive?

'If it's any consolation, I was kept equally in the dark for most of my life. And I detest secrets.'

The last declaration was to gauge her reaction. Sure enough, her gaze shifted away from his.

'Some secrets are better off staying in the dark,' she murmured, so softly he wondered if she'd realised she'd spoken aloud.

He laughed, the sound dark and hollow even to his own ears. 'Only those who seek to justify their subterfuge believe that.'

Her eyes reconnected with his and he was disconcerted by the dark turbulence swirling within. 'Not everything is black and white, Maceo. Some things are out of your control. Some secrets have the power to rip families apart.'

Dio, he knew that too well!

'Only if you let them fester. Cut out the rot and what is left will be enough.'

Long moments ticked by before she glanced away. 'When did Luigi and Carlotta meet?' she asked, returning to the subject she seemed obsessed with.

More and more Maceo was convinced that whatever she was hiding was embedded in her past with Luigi.

'They met when she joined the company. According to those who were around, it was so-called "love at first sight".'

Her lips twisted, and Maceo wanted to applaud her for not attempting to conceal her reaction with inane statements.

'Am I a bad person if I say I wish they hadn't met?' she asked in a hushed voice. One that reluctantly touched him.

'No.'

She started at his unexpected answer. Then ploughed ahead. 'He was the only father I'd ever known.'

'And he turned his back on you. Do you intend to hate him for ever?'

Again, she didn't rush to deny the emotion, and the raw pulse of her anguish touched something dead inside him, threatened to rouse it.

'Maybe not. But he left us before he met Carlotta, and I hate not knowing why.'

'Some uncertainties you have to live with.'

'Would the great Maceo Fiorenti accept something like this and just live with it?' she asked.

The weight of his guilt pressed down hard. He'd pushed, created discord, and then lost those dear to him before he'd had the chance to make amends. 'No, he would not.'

That sat between them for a minute. And Maceo didn't exactly detest the sense of kinship that flowed between them.

'How did he die? The newspapers mentioned a car accident...'

He forced a nod, memories crashing in despite his efforts to hold them at bay. 'It happened in Milan. They'd just landed the biggest deal for the company yet. They threw a party to celebrate.'

'They...?'

A muscle ticked in his temple and his blood felt icy cold. 'My parents were in the same car as Luigi and Carlotta. Luigi and my parents died instantly.'

She gasped. 'And Carlotta? Was she badly hurt?'

'She was thrown from the car before impact and hospitalised briefly, but as you know she made a full recovery.'

'At the drinks tonight, someone mentioned you'd once been in an accident too,' Faye said.

Maceo refocused to find her frowning at him.

He tensed. 'I'll give you a free guess as to how I feel about office gossip.'

She shook her head. 'It wasn't gossip. They assumed I knew.'

He straightened from where he'd been lounging against the fireplace. 'Have you had your fill of information about Luigi already? You must have if you're inclined to indulge yourself in asking about me.' He used the silky tone Carlotta had fondly referred to as his *'il inferno'* voice as he sauntered towards Faye, not bothering to hide his displeasure about this new subject.

She'd clearly read his expression accurately, and he watched as a shiver coursed through her. He lifted his glass to his lips to hide his dark satisfaction at her reaction. Of course that all went away when she licked her bottom lip, leaving a wet trail that thickened his blood, left him with an instant raw need to be the one licking that plump flesh. Sucking it into his mouth. Tasting the hell out of it…

'I thought we were just making conversation,' she said.

'No, *cara*,' he drawled. 'But if you want something *else* to occupy you, I can think of much better things than to discuss me,' he offered.

She jumped up, and mineral water spilt over her fingers. Maceo took the glass and set it down. When he faced her again, she took a step back.

'What…what do you think you're doing?'

Si, Maceo. What are *you doing?*

He wasn't breaking his vow. He was simply…

'Satisfying your curiosity,' he said. He lifted a hand and trailed his fingers over her smooth jawline.

Again she shivered. 'No, you're not. You're…annoyed. And you're using this…whatever this is… to hide it. Why?'

He shrugged. 'You have an overactive imagination, Faye. I'm doing nothing except paying you back for indulging yourself with me this morning.'

She snatched in a breath. 'I thought you said it must never happen again?'

'No need to panic, *cara*. Nothing has happened yet.'

'And nothing will,' she blurted.

No, it wouldn't. Because his path was set. No pleasure. No liaisons. No *famiglia*.

But nothing said he couldn't teach this creature a lesson for toying with him. For making him…*want*.

He breathed a curiously satisfied sigh as Faye remained still, allowed him the freedom to experience her silky skin, to feel the blood rushing beneath her pulse that was slowly turning her pink with desire.

The hunger that had taken hold of him since that morning intensified, rampaging through him like a wild animal. Slowly he nudged her chin with his thumb, tilting her head up to his.

'Why the hair colour?' he asked, finally giving in to his curiosity.

'Because it makes me happy.'

Such a simple answer. And yet so alien to him that he froze. When had he done something for the simple reason of pleasing himself? Not since before he'd woken up from hell and found himself inhabiting a nightmare.

'And the henna tattoos and the unconventional clothes? They make you happy too?' he pressed.

'Yes,' she murmured, subtly leaning into his touch.

Maceo didn't think she was aware that she was doing so. Dark satisfaction flared higher within him.

'Life is dreary enough without helping it along with boring clothes.'

'Such a simplistic thing to say,' he answered, but in some deep, dark part of him he acknowledged that he was…endeared to her.

Temporarily.

Faye Bishop had layers he couldn't afford to be sidetracked by. Not when he sensed there were secrets she strove hard to hide.

She shrugged. 'I am what I am.'

He indulged himself in another stroke of her skin. Felt her tremble and his own groin pulsate in response.

'But you're not, *cara*, are you? There is much more hidden beneath, isn't there?'

'I'm not sure exactly what's going on here, Maceo…'

He stepped closer, breathing her in. 'Say my name again,' he commanded.

'Why?'

'Because it pleases me.'

Shame slammed into him at the admission. But he didn't…couldn't…take it back.

'Do you always get what you want?' she asked.

'No, I do not. If I did my family would still be alive.'

The starkness of his answer froze them both and he saw the beginnings of softness in her eyes. He wanted to lap it up and at the same time reject it. He did neither. He simply continued to caress her, the hypnotic forbidden thrill of it seeping deeper into his blood.

'I'm sorry you lost them,' she murmured, with genuine sympathy in her eyes.

He inclined his head, accepting the words but then dismissing them before they wound themselves around places he would swear weren't vulnerable.

She opened her mouth again. And against his better judgment and every vow—perhaps because he was suddenly wary of her expertise in confounding him—he stalled her by the most direct means available to him: lowering his head and kissing her.

This was by no means his first kiss, but it was his first since that moment he'd opened his eyes to a whole new world. A world where his parents were no longer alive. A world where guilt and cruel might-have-beens resided.

One simple touch of her lips and Maceo's senses detonated in an unrelenting force so potent and yet so pure it sent him reeling. She moaned, and the sound only intensified his hunger. Her sweet, supple body swayed into him. He wrapped an arm around her waist, drawing her closer. A gruff sound was unleashed from him as her softness moulded to his hardness.

It was as if he'd been uncaged.

He drank her in, delving deep into her mouth to taste every inch. And how sweet she tasted. Adolescent experiences he could barely recall evaporated from his mind for ever, replaced by this new, mind-bending sensation threatening to overwhelm him.

Faye's scent. Her taste. The soft firmness of her body. All eroded his greatest asset—his control. But even as he assured himself he could wrestle it back, he was also admitting to himself that he'd never felt want like this.

His marriage hadn't been a traditional one. Only he and Carlotta knew their truth. So his need was particularly acute as he fisted Faye's hair, helped himself to another taste of cherry blossom and the pure woman in his arms.

And he would have kept on sampling and indulging if reality had not seeped in like a dark, icy storm.

Was he really doing this? Blithely discarding his vow for the sake of this foolish *temporary* temptation? When the last thing he deserved was *any* form of serenity?

With a control he wrestled extremely hard for, he broke the kiss.

Eyes wide, breath panting, Faye stared up at him, a look of horror slowly etching her face. 'I'm not sure exactly what that was, but—'

'I can spell it out for you or give you another demonstration if you need pointers?' he said, infusing his voice with nonchalance he didn't feel. Maceo had no intention of losing himself like that again, but she didn't need to know it.

She shook her head, sparking an irrational irritation inside him as the look of horror remained on her face, despite feeling a similar sensation at himself.

'I don't want pointers, thank you. What I'd like is to go to bed—if this little game of yours is over?' Without waiting for an answer, she hurried towards the door.

Maceo followed, the decision he'd made at the mausoleum earlier rushing back to him. *Keep her close...safeguard my parents' legacy.*

He watched her climb the sweeping stairs, her bare feet and shapely legs sparking renewed hunger inside him. At the top of the stairs she paused, one hand on the banister, the other clutching her shoes.

It was as if that compulsion in him had reached out and snagged her. Slowly, she looked over her shoulder, eyes watchful. Saying nothing.

Maceo allowed the silence to pulse while thick, dangerous emotions sizzled between them. Then he delivered his final volley. The one he'd savoured with far too much anticipation while he'd awaited her return.

'Just so you know, from Monday you're moving departments.'

She inhaled sharply. 'Excuse me?'

'You can continue your little assignment for R&D, but it's time to switch things up a little. You'll be working directly with me. Who knows? You might catch me in a mood to answer a few more of your questions about Luigi.'

She stared down at him, her mouth working although no sound emerged. Maceo wanted her to storm back down and tackle him about his announcement. To accuse him of dangling the carrot of Luigi to get what he wanted.

Hell, he wanted a great many things—things that should shroud him in shame and guilt. Because even now his lips tingled. He resisted the urge to touch his fingers to them by lifting his glass and draining the last of his drink, his eyes never leaving her face.

Perhaps she saw his internal battle and deemed it wise to maintain a sensible distance.

Maceo wasn't sure how long they stayed like that, locked in a silent war of unwanted arousal. Faye with her sexy shoes dangling from her fingers, her graceful body arched towards him and her indigo eyes unable to detach from his. Him with the animal need that rampaged through him threatening to leap out of control. Only his vow, battered but stalwart, held him in place.

Eventually she nodded jerkily, her tongue darting nervously over her lips. 'Fighting you on this isn't worth my time. I guess I'll just have to count the days until this is all over. Right? Goodnight, Maceo.'

He didn't respond, because every fibre of his being was locked in a battle to stay where he was and not race up the stairs after her.

Not even the discovery half an hour later that Pico had vanished again and was most likely ensconced in Faye's room was enough to shift him from his study.

Winning this skirmish with her was what mattered.

And he intended to win each one.

It was just a kiss.

Funny how, with every forceful repetition of those five words, the weaker their reassurance became. Five days later and what should have been a deep dive into the cocoa and sugar production reports Maceo had asked her to read barely registered. The effect of that kiss—and her feeble insistence that it had had no profound effect on her—resurfaced again and again to shatter her concentration.

Faye stifled a frustrated growl, kicked off her shoes, rose from the sofa where the reports were strewn and stretched her limbs. But as she strolled to the window of her new office next to Maceo's she darkly acknowledged that stiff limbs weren't her problem.

Her problem was *that kiss.*

Her problem was the dark magic of Maceo's ferocious passion…how easily he'd overcome her resistance.

Most of all her problem was her own stunned realisation that whatever had gone before was nothing compared to the thrill of what she'd experienced.

He'd kissed as if he desired her. As if she mattered. As if he would have expired if he hadn't devoured her.

Because he doesn't know!

And she, momentarily forgetting every valid reason why she shouldn't…*couldn't*…give in to such base emotions, had yearned for more with every cell in her body.

But when the reminder had rammed through the fog of her desire and brought her to her senses, Maceo had seemed just as stricken as she felt.

Because he'd only recently buried his wife…

There it was again. That stinging sensation. It was almost as if she was…*jealous.* It was irrational. And shaming. Because with every day spent in this place she learned that Carlotta Caprio-Fiorenti had been just shy of a saint. She'd been devoted to Luigi, and then to Maceo. She'd possessed a deep sense of family—as evidenced by her brothers' prominent positions in the company.

Had that been the drive behind Carlotta's effort to reach out to Faye despite her less than warm reception? The bite of guilt was damning and unwelcome. Perhaps because through all of this turbulence she'd still held back from asking Maceo about that picture. About Pietro and who he had been to Luigi and his parents.

She hadn't come across anything else about him, despite scrutinising the countless Fiorenti and Caprio pictures displayed all over the villa, and secretly searching the library from top to bottom for another hidden picture.

A frustrated sound bubbled up from her throat.

'The reports are that challenging?' a deep, sardonic voice said from behind her.

She spun around, a small gasp leaving her lips. Maceo stood in the centre of the room, a solid, riveting figure who made it impossible to acknowledge anything else in the vicinity. With the sun long set, and only a couple of lamps illuminating the interior of her office, the play of light and darkness lent him an even more enigmatic aura, triggering a sort of hypnotic absorption that made her heart thump faster as he filled the room, taking up vital space and oxygen.

'Not at all.' She strove for equanimity and breathed a sigh of relief when she achieved it.

His head tilted a fraction, that assessing gaze zeroing in on her vulnerable spots—which she was discovering were many when it came to this man.

'Then what's the problem?'

'Nothing I can't handle,' she said with false nonchalance. Because he was coming closer, and her gaze was doing that thing where it remained glued to him no matter how much she tried to resist.

Maceo didn't have the same problem, evidently. His gaze veered away to skate over the papers, then the shoes she'd abandoned some time in the last hour. For some reason his eyes remained riveted on the red-soled heels for charged moments before, sliding his hands into his pockets, he redirected his scrutiny to her.

'Pick two,' he threw out, a deep throb in his voice.

Faye dragged her gaze from the play of dark blended wool over his strong thighs. 'Two…?' she echoed, in an alarmingly husky voice.

He jerked his chin at the reports. 'Are you up to date on the sustainability projects with our growers?' he asked, instead of answering her question.

'Yes.'

She was stunned by what she'd read. She'd dealt with enough supposedly community-minded companies in her bid to secure funding for New Paths and similar women's shelters to know that not all conglomerates were willing to spread their wealth. But Casa di Fiorenti went above and beyond in supporting the farmers whose products it bought. Free grants and sharing resources had increased profit on the ground level—an unprecedented outcome that had seen its competitors scrambling to save face by emulating the multi-billion-euro company.

'And?' Maceo prompted, alerting her to the fact that she'd got lost in the wonder of it all.

'And whoever had the idea to give the farmers the tools they need to increase their output deserves a medal. Several medals.'

A wry smile ghosted over his lips. 'You have Luigi to thank for that,' he said, approaching her where she stood.

Warmth and bewilderment twisted through her. 'He did this?'

Maceo nodded. 'He set the ball rolling long before it was fashionable to give without expecting something in return.'

Then why? her heart screamed. Why had he shown such kindness and consideration to others but deserted her and her mother so heartlessly? Had their damage and stigma been too much for him?

Faye barely managed to stop herself from making another sound—this one an echo of the pain ripping through her. Instead, she focused on the conversation, aware of Maceo's incisive eyes fixed on her.

'But you kept it going? These labs set up to provide vital technology to help the farmers were put in place only a few years ago.'

'It made good business sense to keep on enabling them to self-sustain. But the legacy is Luigi's.'

Faye wondered if he'd come here to tell her this.

Since Friday night he'd been dropping tiny morsels about her stepfather into their conversations. On Monday he'd told her Luigi had backed his father against the board's resistance to hire their first female CFO. Tuesday he had revealed that Luigi and Rafael had been childhood friends from their first day in kindergarten, and that Luigi had taken Maceo on his first sky-diving adventure on his sixteenth birthday—much to his parents' dismay.

While each revelation was a dagger to her heart—because the evidence was stacking up that Luigi had withheld crucial parts of his life, and ultimately left because of her and her mother's shortcomings—Faye had begun eagerly anticipating these visits and revelations from Maceo.

Was it because she hardly saw him otherwise? Because a secret, entirely foolish part of her hoped for a repetition of what had happened on Friday night, even though she knew it was a dangerous, insane route to take?

She pushed the intrusive questions away. 'Thank you for telling me. I'm still not sure whether it helps me or not.'

He stared at her contemplatively before he answered. 'I'm merely providing the information. What you choose to do with it is your decision.'

A knot of bitterness slipped past her guard. 'But you're only telling me the good bits. Not whether he ever let you down. Did he ever lose his temper? Make a bad decision?'

A flicker resembling pain dulled his eyes before he blinked it away. 'Luigi was flawed, like most people. Would my recounting his mistakes make you feel better?'

Yes.

She bit her tongue, suddenly self-conscious, and retraced her barefoot steps to the sofa, aware with each one how small she was in contrast to Maceo's towering frame. How dishevelled and worn around the edges she looked compared to his immaculate appearance. Under the lamplight his hair gleamed, neat and pristine, his tie was perfectly knotted and his *GQ*-cover-ready Italian designer shoes were polished to within an inch of their life.

To occupy herself, so she didn't gawp at him some more, Faye picked up the nearest document. 'You wanted me to pick two—but you didn't say two what.'

'Two production sites you'd like to visit, to see for yourself the work Luigi started,' he said.

The words ignited something peculiar that burrowed beneath her skin and sparked her blood. And as they sank in she forgot she wasn't going to stare or appreciate the masculine perfection as he drew closer.

She met his potent tawny gaze full-on and momentarily lost the ability to breathe. 'I… What? You want me to visit a production site with you?' she parroted.

He stopped an arm's length away and shrugged.

'It's a twice-yearly opportunity we organise for our employees. The last one was two months ago, so this will be a special trip with just the two of— *Cieli sopra!*'

The sudden tightness of his voice, charged with powerful emotion, made Faye's heart miss several beats. Puzzled, she followed his gaze, and flames stormed through her as she caught sight of what had snagged his attention—the bra she'd discarded an hour ago in a fit of frustrated discomfort. She'd thought she'd shoved the frivolous bit of lingerie deep into her bag, but apparently it had been dislodged when she'd kicked off her shoes.

Now Maceo stared at the bright red scrap of lace as if it personally offended his every sensibility. His hand darted to the breast pocket of his jacket, before veering sharply away as if stung.

'Do you make a habit of disrobing in the office?'

His voice was hoarse, throbbing with a beat that resonated deep inside her pelvis.

Faye nudged her bag with her foot. All that achieved was to drag the bra into clearer view. 'I… Of course not. It's after hours. I thought you'd left. That I was alone.'

She chanced a glance at him, and discovered that for some reason her response had made his eyes blaze even fiercer.

'And my presence is the only reason you'd keep your underwear on?'

Despite her burning face, she glared at him. 'I

didn't mean that and you know it. Don't twist my words, please.' She surged forward with cringe-worthy gracelessness and tucked the bra out of sight, excruciatingly aware of his laser focus boring into her.

'Are you done here?' he demanded tightly.

She nodded stiffly. 'Just about.'

'Good—then you'll leave with me.'

'Oh, please. This isn't some period drama. You don't need to protect my honour.' Especially when her very origins were severely questionable.

'Perhaps not. But I find myself needing to ensure that no other man sees you like this.'

The low, terse revelation, writhing with possessiveness, detonated between them, rendering them both immobile and unable to do anything but stare, aghast, at each other. Or at least Faye was certain that was how she was looking at him. Because the stormy emotions coursing through her made her want to fling herself at him, regardless of the words coming out of his mouth.

'Chauvinist, much?' she snapped.

He let her indictment bounce off his broad shoulders without so much as a wince. 'I care very little about how I appear, *cara*. I care very much about returning you to the villa, *pronto*, before you take off another item of clothing.'

Faye got the impression that he wasn't going to budge from her office. And, much to her dismay, she discovered she *wanted* to go with him. Wanted to remain in his company despite the wild sizzle and crackle between them. Despite the fact that her body was still caught in a maelstrom of sensations, the epicentre of which was the super-sensitive budding of her nipples and the flames licking through her pelvis.

Despite every inch of him proclaiming the danger of remaining for one more second in his company, she slipped her shaky feet into her high heels and caught up her bag. 'Okay. Let's go.'

He caught her wrist in his large hand and led her to his private lift. Downstairs, as if he'd commanded it by telepathy, the few employees working late stayed well clear of them. When they reached his speedboat, Maceo barely acknowledged the pilot's greeting.

He planted himself in front of her, shielding her from the view of his driver, his wide body blocking out the worst of the breeze. He continued to keep hold of her arm, his gaze never once straying from her face.

'So…your choices?' he asked stiffly after a minute, barely raising his voice.

She looked up. His gaze caught hers and held it captive. Breathless, she watched it linger, hot and hungry, on her lips before dropping to her chest.

A shocking phenomenon occurred just then.

Far from folding her arms to hide his effect on her, Faye retained her pose, felt her breasts suddenly heavy and needy, her hands dangling by her sides as she sorted through her thoughts to answer his question. *Choices... Site visits...*

'Oh…um… St Lucia. And Ghana.'

He nodded. 'We'll leave this weekend—after the party.'

Under different circumstances she would have reeled at the novelty of everything that had happened in the last few weeks—her inheritance, the luxurious splendour of the villa, the job she found herself enjoying more with each day…hell, even her new clothes. But, while she'd known from the first that Maceo Fiorenti was a formidable man, the almost conceited way he wielded his power continually left her slack-jawed—not that he'd noticed, since he pretty much did as he pleased with little regard for anyone else.

'How long will we be gone?' she asked, struggling to handle yet another twist in this roller coaster.

His gaze sharpened, his sensual lips momentarily flattening. 'Ten days—perhaps more. Already missing your clubbing friends?'

'Believe it or not, I do have people who're interested in my travel plans.'

His hard look eased. 'Your parents?'

She sucked in a breath, then reminded herself that Maceo didn't know her history. 'My mother.'

'And your father? Is he—'

'Not in the picture. Never has been. Never will be,' she insisted, but that sickening sensation gripped her gut so tightly she had to force herself to breathe carefully through it or risk giving herself away.

She didn't notice that goosebumps had broken out on her flesh until his hands slid up and down her arms in a contemplative caress. A different sort of shiver assailed her then, almost but not quite nudging that sickening feeling aside.

'Such a strong reaction—'

'And entirely none of your business,' she injected forcefully, hoping he'd drop the subject.

Thankfully he did, although his gaze raked her face repeatedly before he lifted a hand to tuck a coil of runaway hair behind her ear.

Perhaps it was relief and gratitude that made her turn into his touch. Or perhaps she'd taken complete leave of her senses tonight.

Whatever it was, she gasped when he cupped her cheek, his hand hot and possessive and electrifying enough to make her pulse race faster.

'Faye?'

'Hmm?'

'A body as sensitive as yours shouldn't go unarmoured,' he rasped, his voice low and deep and entirely too dangerous, too *intimate*, for her peace of mind.

A very feminist part of her bristled. 'Because any unwanted attention I receive from the opposite sex will be entirely *my* fault?' she challenged.

One corner of his mouth twisted mirthlessly. 'Because whatever male you eventually belong to will find the idea of you in this state—when he can't do a single thing about it without causing scandal—completely maddening. Enough to risk him committing indecent crimes.'

Whatever male you eventually belong to...

Part of her wanted to laugh. The other part, that had retreated, horrified and bruised, from Matt's callous condemnation, writhed in fresh anguish. She would never *belong* to anyone. Because no one would ever see beyond the stain that marked her.

'Thank you for your concern, but you needn't worry it'll ever come to that,' she said.

Primal fire brimmed in his eyes for heart-pounding seconds. Then his hand stroked over his jacket pocket again, his expression growing a touch bewildered before his features shuttered.

He kept hold of her. Helped her off the speedboat when they arrived at Villa Serenita. Tersely dismissed the staff who approached. And when she refused dinner, on account of having already had a light supper in her office, he walked her to her bedroom door, where he bade her a low, charged goodnight.

But not before his laser gaze rested one last time on her bag. On her hair. And finally on her lips before, turning abruptly, he strode away.

Leaving her with the bewildering sensation that she'd narrowly escaped a seismic event.

CHAPTER SIX

FAYE TOLD HERSELF it was entirely coincidental that the silver-threaded white bohemian dress she chose on Saturday was designed to be worn braless. She wasn't tempting fate—never mind one Maceo Fiorenti.

Since their intense interaction on Wednesday he'd reverted to ignoring her existence, not even dropping by to dangle morsels of information like he'd done the previous days. Work-related communications, including information about their trip to St Lucia tomorrow morning, had been transmitted via Bruno.

It was also Bruno who'd informed her of the smart-chic dress code that had prompted her dress selection for the party.

All day the villa had been a whirlwind of preparation. From the vantage point of her mosaic-tiled terrace she'd watched staff stringing fairy lights into the cypress trees dotted around the grounds, landscapers primping every inch of the gardens until the roses and poppies seemed to bloom brighter, and long tables with pristine silverware being set up at various corners of the grounds, gleaming.

Thirty minutes ago the first of the guests had started arriving. She'd head downstairs just as soon as she'd calmed the turbo-charged butterflies in her belly...

She started as a firm knock sounded. Blowing out a nervous breath, she slipped gaily coloured poppy-shaped hoop earrings into her lobes, put on red platform heels, then crossed to the door.

Maceo stood on the threshold, much as he had on Wednesday night, but with a much more measured look. Which changed when he took in her attire. He looked…thunderstruck. A terse Italian expletive was ejected from between his lips, and one hand crept up to his nape.

Faye watched his every reaction with something like lightning in her veins. Then, equally enthralled, she watched him wrestle every scrap of emotion under control, until only a smouldering fire remained in his eyes.

'Are you ready?' he enquired, his voice nowhere as smooth as normal.

'Provided I pass muster, yes.'

The look he levelled at her threatened to burn her to a cinder. 'You are well aware of just how you look, *signorina*. Far be it from me to pile even more compliments on your beautiful head.'

Her insides dipped alarmingly. She would have responded with a offhand remark had he not held out his arm to her. Mildly stupefied, she took it. Let him lead her down the hallway towards the stairs.

'Have you given any further thought to selling me your share?' he asked, with a flippancy she was sure was fabricated.

'Was that why you came up to my room? To make inroads into getting what you want?'

Why that made his jaw clench, Faye had no idea.

'I always get what I want, *arcobaleno*. It's simply a matter of timing.'

'Yours or mine?' She strove for a waspish tone to defuse the pleasure moving through her at his endearment.

His lips twisted sardonically. 'Mine, of course.'

'You know I'm tempted to refuse to sell to you now, just on principle, don't you?'

'But you'll give it the careful consideration it deserves and conclude that you're far too sensible to do that, *si*?' he queried mockingly.

'Just for that, I'm inclined to string you along for the foreseeable future.'

His face hardened. 'Tomorrow is never guaranteed. Remember that, Faye.'

Thrown into a pit of uncertainty at the sombre warning, she remained silent.

When they arrived on the terrace he nodded curtly, then turned away as several dozen guests approached him. A blessing in disguise that allowed her to blend into the background, she told herself.

Snagging a glass of tonic water, she made small talk with the guests who spoke English, and smiled through her halting Italian with those who didn't. When Alberto spotted her and wove his way towards her, Faye sighed in relief.

He designated himself her guide, introducing her to everyone in their vicinity until her head spun from trying to recall names.

She was helping herself to a delicious bite of

lemon chicken when Stefano and Francesco Castella approached. Thus far she'd had no personal interaction with Carlotta's brothers, but she'd seen them around the office…noted their calculating glances.

They reached her, and she saw Maceo's head jerk up from where he was engrossed in conversation across the terrace. Narrowed eyes flicked from her to the brothers, returning to hers for several moments before he looked away.

Despite their inconsequential small talk, Faye sensed the Castella brothers were assessing her, probing her for weakness. Beside her, Alberto stiffened at each seemingly casual phrase they uttered. And she sensed the many glances Maceo threw her way while the brothers lingered.

When they eventually left, she frowned at Alberto's sigh of relief.

'What was all that?' Faye asked, slowly expelling a calming breath.

'Nothing you should waste your time on,' Alberto reassured her, although his faint frown indicated otherwise. 'Those two are…*drammatico*.'

Faye bit her tongue against pressing for further elaboration. This was a party, after all. Although judging by the thunder on Maceo's face when he glanced her way her once more, enjoyment wasn't high on his list.

Not for a single moment in his life had Maceo been so racked with indecision.

Stay close or retreat.

Give in to her demands or pretend she didn't exist.

Every course of action reaped the same outcome—the intensifying of that hunger that had taken root within him, awakening needs he'd suppressed because seeking pleasure of any kind was an insult to his parents' memory.

But since that kiss he'd been bracingly reminded that he was a man. With a man's needs. And Faye was very much a woman. A woman with a great many secrets that might very well prove detrimental to him. To the legacy his parents had died safeguarding.

But a woman, nevertheless.

Out of sight or in his presence, wearing one of her outrageous outfits with that *arcobaleno* hair, she *haunted* him.

He sucked in a slow, steadying breath. Which immediately betrayed him by arriving with her delicate scent. He attempted to concentrate on the conversation he was having, although he didn't need much brain power to glean that it was skewed towards another sycophantic display.

Faye would never stray into sycophancy. She's probably never even come across the word.

She neither cared about impressing him nor elevating herself in his eyes, the way every other guest here strained to. And, despite his less than subtle statements on Wednesday night, she hadn't condemned him to the primitive, sexist junkyard where he probably belonged.

Whatever male you eventually belong to...

Santa cielo! There had been no other male in his thoughts besides himself when he'd uttered those ridiculous words. And, *Dio lo aiuti*, he'd felt every one of them in his very bones. Had experienced a hot, powerful throb of primal possessiveness that had made him question his sanity.

The same sensation had assaulted him when she'd opened her door to him earlier, wearing a dress that had shredded his control. Only a desperate summoning of that framed list, that soul-shaking vow, had stopped him from succumbing to his savage hunger. He didn't *deserve* relief of any kind. Especially not with Luigi's stepdaughter. Although he was beginning to suspect Carlotta's hand in this new and singular torment he was currently experiencing...

Maceo was aware he was fast reaching the end of this particular rope. That soon he would throw another log into the inferno he battled each day. One he suspected might well test his very mettle—

'Is everything satisfactory, *signor*?' asked his Latin American senior executive.

Maceo unclenched his jaw long enough to deliver an excuse tempered with a stiff smile, before removing himself from the tedious conversation.

Instantly, husky laughter reached his ears...

curled around his senses, held on tight and demanded attention.

Faye.

With a compulsion he deeply resented, he glanced across his landscaped gardens. There she was, surrounded by a clutch of admirers.

Telling himself he should be satisfied that Stefano and Francesco had made themselves scarce didn't work as his feet propelled him to her. As the bare expanse of her smooth back dissected by the thinnest of twin straps made him swallow a groan.

To their credit, her admirers dispersed as he approached, leaving them alone in the shadow of a cypress tree. The sun hadn't quite set, and the encroaching gloom before the lights came on perfectly suited Maceo's mood.

'You have a face like thunder again,' Faye murmured. 'Tell me… Your dislike of me—it goes beyond your role as executor of Carlotta's will, doesn't it?' She raised defiant eyes to his.

Dio mio, she was truly fearless. And somehow he couldn't find it in himself to be annoyed by it any longer.

'If you must know, I detest people who expect handouts for doing nothing. But perhaps in your case there's valid cause to give you a pass.'

Her mouth dropped open. 'There is?'

He shrugged. And before she could respond to the words he hadn't intended to speak, he ploughed ahead. 'What were you discussing with Stefano and Francesco?'

Her eyes widened, knowledge dawning in their indigo depths. 'They're the reason for your hang-ups, aren't they?'

Partly.

'Answer the question, if you please.'

She sipped her drink leisurely before she answered. 'They tried to be coy about it, but I think they were prying into what I am to you.'

'And?'

'And I didn't give them the satisfaction of an answer. I reckoned if you want them to know, you'll tell them.'

Her unexpected loyalty stunned him. *'Grazie.'*

'What did they do? And, before you deny it, know that I have eyes, Maceo.'

Why did his name on her lips thrill him so? And why wasn't he telling her to mind her own business?

'Besides making Carlotta's life a misery at every opportunity?' he said.

She frowned. 'Carlotta? I thought this was about you. It felt…personal.'

Although for the life of him he couldn't decipher why, he found himself elaborating. 'After the accident, they and the rest of the board members tried to take the company away from her. They pulled every trick in the book, from declaring her incompetent to manipulating her grief. They even attempted blackmail.'

'Then why are they still here, employed by Casa di Fiorenti?' *By you*, her tone suggested.

'Because she was kind-hearted. To Carlotta, family meant everything.'

His neutrality failed when he heard the rough edge of guilt and bitterness in his own voice.

'You don't share the sentiment?' Faye observed.

Secrets he wished he didn't possess clawed at his insides. 'Not when that family is intent on doing you harm, no.'

'The company was yours too. Didn't they come after you?'

'I happened to be…indisposed at the time.'

'Indisposed?'

His lips twisted. 'The small matter of being in a coma and unable to defend myself.'

She paled and sucked in a sharp breath. 'You were in a *coma*?'

Maceo was surprised the office gossips hadn't already divulged that information.

'Oh, my God, Maceo…'

Did she know she'd clutched his arm? That her grip tightened by the second? A throb of guilty pleasure beat through him along with the shame, because he liked her touch far too much to tell her. To remind himself why he shouldn't allow it.

'How—' She gasped as enlightenment arrived. 'You were in the same accident?' she whispered.

'*Si*, I was.' Something moved through him—an

awakening of that deep pain. That profound regret. And the guilt. *Always the guilt.*

'What…? How did you survive?'

He shrugged. 'According to witnesses, I was thrown clear too, before the car went off the road. I wasn't as lucky as Carlotta, though. I suffered head injuries and slipped into a coma.'

One he hadn't come out of for over a year.

Her breath emerged shakily. He wanted to devour it. To absorb every ounce of emotion she could spare, hoard it like a miser for those dark days ahead when the reality that he was truly alone threatened to drive him insane.

Did he deserve even that? No, he didn't. And yet he couldn't help himself.

'Does your heart grow soft for me, *cara*?' he queried, yearning for another morsel to take his mind off his bleak future.

She exhaled, another shaky breath that drew him like a siren song. 'I'd be heartless not to feel for anyone who goes through something like that.'

'But I'm not "anyone", am I, Faye?'

Several expressions chased across her face, charged by the dark magic that weaved around them. 'No, you're not. But you deserve the same consideration.'

Her attempt to put him in his place unsettled him. 'Is that all I deserve?' he pressed, giving in to the urge to stroke that smooth, silky cheek, to brush his thumb over lips that tasted as sweet as he suspected heaven tasted.

He knew he should stop. Knew he was letting himself down. But, *mio Dio*, this woman made him weak. And he'd been fighting for so long…

He'd never attributed any lofty connotations to his sexual circumstances. The decision he'd taken over a decade ago had been rooted in loyalty and the need to honour his parents' memory. He'd vowed not to chase pleasure or contentment when his parents lay dead because he'd acted as judge, jury and executioner.

Nothing had changed. His demons raged as virulently as ever, demanding his continued sacrifice. So why was denying himself now so challenging? Why, for the first time in a decade, did he want to fall short of his own goals?

'I'm not sure how…what you mean…'

'Aren't you?'

'Maceo…'

He parried. She retreated.

Their silent little dance had led them behind a larger cypress tree, farther away from curious eyes. Capturing her soft nape, lowering his head and taking those luscious lips with his in that moment felt deliciously simple. And yet life-altering in a way that shook through him.

She moaned and clung harder to him. The sweet sound of her whimper tore a reciprocal sound from within him—a vocal manifestation of the hunger clawing through him. A hunger *she'd* stoked from the first moment he'd set eyes on her. A hunger he knew deep in his bones would be just as tough to wrestle as his demons.

Later. When this temporary madness had eased.

He nudged her against the tree, exhaling in satisfaction as her soft curves moulded to him. It was almost as if she had been made for him, if one believed in such whimsy.

He most certainly didn't. This was simply a combination of chemicals, aligned to trigger base instincts. Nothing more. He would walk away as soon as this insanity was dispensed with.

He spiked his fingers into her hair, angled her face up for a deeper kiss. A deeper taste.

And felt her hands on his chest.

Pushing him away.

Maceo levered himself away, disbelief dripping ice and reality into his veins, reminding of where he was. *Who* he was.

'Stop. I… I can't,' she said, her voice husky with arousal but firm enough to push him back another step.

While he'd been lost in her allure the lights had come on. A metaphor for his shameful actions, perhaps? Too late, his hand drifted to his breastbone. But of course he'd left the list in his bedroom. Because he didn't want to be reminded of it? A deeper shame crawled over his skin as the answer arrived in the throbbing of his groin.

'Maceo?'

'Hurry along then, *bellissimo arcobaleno*. Consider your reprieve granted.'

Her eyes widened and her lips worked as if she would object. But a second later she turned her back and walked away. Leaving him in a far greater torment than he'd wrestled with only an hour ago. Because, as he'd suspected, even the simple act of watching her walk away challenged his every vow. Threatened to erode the foundations of the belief that had guided him so steadily for a decade.

His turmoil was nowhere near battened down when he rejoined the party and played host with forced alacrity. And when the last guest had departed and he went upstairs, not towards his own suite but in *her* direction, he told himself it was because he needed to face this new demon head-on.

His knock was loud and rough, echoing the sensations inside him.

She opened the door wearing another concoction of bright colours, this time a thigh-skimming nightie that left the expanse of her long, magnificent legs on display.

Maceo swallowed a thick sound he was sure stemmed from this woman's torment of him and watched her wide indigo eyes latch defiantly on to his.

'Is there something you need, Maceo?'

Diavolo, si. He wanted this madness to end. *Pronto.* He wanted his belief in the promises he'd made to remain unshaken, to accept his solitary state, to remain the sole survivor left behind to honour the sacrifices of his family.

He most certainly didn't want his head crowded with thoughts of this woman. To be tortured with elusive glimpses of what stepping off the path he'd chosen for himself might look like.

So he forced his hands to remain at his sides, his shoulder braced against the doorjamb as he cast an indolent eye into her suite. 'Pico. Where is he?'

She blinked in bewilderment. 'You're here about the dog?'

'*Si. My* dog. Whom you've commandeered for far too long. Where is he?'

He gave a low whistle. From behind her shoulder, fully ensconced in her bed and looking infinitely content with his lot, Pico raised his head. He proceeded to eye Maceo warily, warning him not to ruin his good fortune.

Maceo was both ashamed and irritated by his intense jealousy of his pet.

'He's comfortable where he is,' Faye stated—as if Maceo didn't have eyes.

'That may be so, but I recall giving specific instructions that you were to stay away from him.'

She huffed in annoyance. 'Are you *really* here to tell me off about Pico?'

With a compulsion he couldn't resist, he reached out and stroked the irresistible smoothness of her neck. 'Yes,' he answered truthfully. Gruffly. 'But there's another matter that needs attention…'

His hand caressed lower, to the sweet juncture where her neck met her shoulder.

She shivered, but remained bold. Ferociously staring him down. 'Is there?'

'*Si*, and I think you know, Faye. You know that I can't seem to fight this need to taste you again since I discovered once wasn't enough,' he said, aware that his voice was almost accusatory.

His candour seemed to disarm her, if only for a moment. But he gloried in that second when her skin flushed and her lips parted. When her breathing grew rapid and beneath the satin sheen of her nightgown her nipples pebbled.

'And I think you want to taste me too.'

'What do you want me to say to that?' she asked.

Her eyes grew heavy as he stepped into the room, but she didn't retreat. Her fire only beckoned him, pulled him to his doom.

'Deny me, Faye,' he growled, lowering his head because he couldn't *not* draw closer to the perfection of her lips. Couldn't *not* inhale the sweet scent of cherry blossom and arousal blooming from her. 'Perhaps it's best for both of us if you do.'

He had no intention of indulging in immersion therapy, but perhaps sensory deprivation was what he needed. All the same he held his breath, his insides churning with something close to trepidation. Because suddenly a *no* seemed like the worst possible declaration.

Fire sparked from her eyes. 'You've decided I'm

to be your next plaything when you don't even like me. Why should I make this game easy for you?'

He bit back a grim smile, stroked his fingers over the soft skin at her throat, revelling in the rush of her pulse beneath his touch.

'You're mistaken about a few things. For starters, *playing* is the last thing on my mind, *arcobaleno*. Secondly, there are a great many things two people can indulge in without the prerequisite to *like* each other.'

A shocked little laugh left her lips. 'Are you serious?'

He looked her square in the eyes, tempted to show her the demons he was ignoring for this stolen moment. 'Exceedingly. You want me to prove it? Tell me right now, Faye. Do you *like* me?'

Her lashes swept down for a moment, then her eyes clashed with his once more. 'Answering that one way or another will give you an unfair advantage.'

He laughed, to his own surprise registering that he was enjoying this exchange. Perhaps immersion therapy was exactly what he needed. Because holding back from devouring her was crucifying him.

'The only one with an unfair advantage is you,' he said.

'Why is that?'

'Because right in this moment you hold all the damn power. Take it, Faye, if you dare,' he taunted.

Her eyes narrowed. Then, with an aggrieved hiss, she launched herself at him.

Maceo speared his fingers into her soft, silky hair, tugging her none too gently that last vital inch into his body. Then he walked her back soundlessly across the carpet towards the wide, inviting expanse of her rumpled bed.

With a groan torn from his soul he devoured her, teeth, tongue and lips sampling every inch of her mouth. Giddily, he felt her hands on him, equally exploring, equally urgent. Demanding everything he wanted to give.

Absently, he heard a tiny affronted yelp, then a thump as Pico relocated himself to the floor.

Maceo's smile of triumph was lost somewhere in the deep kiss he demanded from the warm, tempting woman beneath him. The woman whose secrets and shadows should repel him, whose very presence in his life should reinforce his pledge but instead was shattering it.

Besides his vow, the other reason for his turbulent emotions rammed home.

Diavolo, he didn't like to think of himself as special, but he knew that, despite the circumstances, his situation was unique. A thirty-year-old male without a single true sexual experience belonged in a museum. Or in the depths of some faith-based tome. Not strutting about wearing Italian silk and juggling the challenges of a billion-euro business.

The more reality trickled in, the more the possibility of Faye cracking the titanium shell of his vow grew. Until experiencing his *first*…experiencing *her*…was all that occupied his mind.

Another thing he was discovering was that when Faye was in his arms the demons quietened. He wasn't idiotic enough to believe they would recede indefinitely. But the temporary respite was…intoxicating. Enough to make him yearn for it.

He would pay the price for his selfishness later, when the true depths of his desolation came crashing in. But for now…

'For what it's worth, *cara*, my coming here wasn't an easy decision,' he drawled against her swollen lips.

She stiffened instantly, and he wanted to curse himself to the darkest depths of hell.

'Thank you for that. But—'

'Let me take a wild guess. It won't be happening?' he said.

The dryness in his voice could have started a brush fire. But it was nothing compared to the clamouring in his head as his demons rushed back, mocking his desperation to escape.

'No, it *won't*,' she stressed, pushing at his shoulders.

It didn't help that her voice shook. Or that uncertainty wavered across her face.

But little by little, her resolve hardened. Maceo saw it and despised it, because he was jealous of his inability to feel the same way. To stop himself from reaching out for more when he didn't deserve it.

More than a little bewildered, he laughed under

his breath. Perhaps this was another hard lesson he needed to learn.

'Pico stays with me,' she stated, her chin once again tilted in defiance as he rose from the bed and paced away from temptation.

Dio mio, her ferocity sparked a fire inside him. One he wanted to burn in. 'And who are *you* to dictate such a thing?'

'I'm the one he comes to when he misses his mistress. I'm the one he follows around, despite your unreasonable orders. The one he knows will give him the affection he needs.'

Jealousy seared harder, as did the chasm of desolation inside him. 'Did you ever stop to think I have valid reasons for those orders? He'll most likely grow attached to you, believing you will fill the void, when that couldn't be further from the truth. You have experienced what it feels like to be abandoned, if your emotional outbursts about Luigi are to be believed. And yet you would visit it upon another creature?'

Her keen eyes rested on his face. 'Are we talking about Pico or you, Maceo?' she demanded softly.

That peculiar trepidation tightened his chest. He opened his mouth, intent on a brusque denial. But it died in his throat because he was aware that some of his words might stem from a place he didn't like to examine very often.

'You think you know me that well?' he asked gruffly instead.

'You've lost your family in hard circumstances.

If I were you, I'd be devastated too. And I'd be terribly afraid of getting attached. To anything or anyone. But—'

'But nothing. We're not talking about me,' he interjected, alarm bells clanging because she was hitting far too close to home. 'We're discussing Pico.'

Hurt wavered across her face before her chin rose higher. 'He'll adapt.'

'Will he? Or is that another foolish wish? A way to absolve yourself of guilt because you might be leaving a scar on a recently bereaved soul?'

Dio mio, could he hold a starker mirror up to himself?

Her gaze dropped before boldly meeting his. 'You say that as if he won't have you when I'm gone. Surely having more people to love is better than having none?'

That shell inside him fractured again, leaching needs that would betray his parents' memory. But, as hard as he tried, Maceo couldn't find the strength to seal it. 'Be very careful, Faye.'

He expected her customary feisty response, but a look that closely resembled sadness shrouded her face. 'I will be, Maceo. I always am.'

She turned away. Dismissed him.

Maceo left her room, leaving his triumphant dog behind, and puzzled for the dozenth time why another encounter with Faye Bishop had left him feeling as if he'd grappled with a cyclone and lost, when only recently he'd vowed to win…

CHAPTER SEVEN

If Capri was a cool and sophisticated haven, St Lucia was a sultry, tropical paradise.

The lush vegetation, exotic birds and the sheer profusion of colour seemed almost too good to be true. But then for the last handful of weeks Faye had felt as if she was living in a lucid dream. One of heightened emotion and intense drama, mainly in the form of the man seated next to her in the air-conditioned Jeep with tinted windows, his eyes shielded by a pair of designer sunglasses as they drove away from his private airstrip.

The long flight from Italy to St Lucia had been surreal in itself. Because of course she'd been introduced to another level of affluence in the form of the Fiorenti private jet, equipped with every item of luxury imaginable. And, whether she'd been ensconced in the living area or—in a futile bid to come to terms with the previous night's episode with Maceo, during which she'd skated even closer to danger—retreating to an area that had turned out to be Maceo's personal cinema room, the flight attendants had been a discreet glance away, ready to cater to her every whim.

Not that she'd been tempted to request anything beyond refreshments. She'd been entirely consumed by their interaction from the night before.

Was still consumed by it.

Whereas Maceo seemed to harbour zero qualms about how things had ended.

There'd been no censure, just a long, sizzling, assessing look at the breakfast table. Since then she'd caught him staring contemplatively at her. It wasn't so much as if he was trying to work her out. It was more an inkling that he was already halfway to plundering the heart of her secret.

But from the moment they'd taken off, the powerful CEO had resumed his role. He'd been all about Casa di Fiorenti business, apprising her of their itinerary, which included sailing to two plantations via his yacht. She'd questioned the use of that mode of transport, to be curtly informed that it was so he could travel and work at the same time.

A part of her envied his skilful ability to proceed as normal, while the major part revisited the incident in her suite for the hundredth time.

Yes, she'd disgracefully jumped him. And, yes, the torrid kiss had been sublime. But Faye had become increasingly preoccupied with the conversation *after* she'd pulled the brakes.

The subtext had seemed…monumental. The look on Maceo's face had been an arresting tableau of regret, guilt, pain and fury. Just what had happened to him? And why couldn't she put the incident out of her mind?

As if triggered by the unasked question, his laser-powered gaze flicked to her and she realised he'd spoken. 'I'm sorry, what?'

One sardonic eyebrow lifted. 'We have arrived. I'd leave you to your daydreaming, but I don't think you'd appreciate the heat once I turn the engine off. So…are you coming?'

'Of course I'm—' She looked past him to the structure they'd parked in front of, and was thrown into yet another realm of awe.

'Dear God, do the Fiorentis do anything approaching normal?'

'I don't quite catch your meaning,' he replied, plucking his sunglasses off to slip them into his pocket.

Her gaze darted back to him, her face flaming when she realised she'd spoken out loud. Brazening it out, she flicked a hand at the jaw-dropping house basking in the late-afternoon golden sunlight. 'I mean this…this impossible dream of a house.'

'I take it you like it?' he enquired drolly.

She snorted. 'That's like asking a racing car driver if he likes speed.'

One corner of the mouth she'd become intimately acquainted with last night lifted, lending him a rakish, almost boyish look that softened the dark edges of his demeanour. Heat swirled through her belly as two things struck her—firstly, that she'd never seen him truly smile, and secondly that she was terrified to contemplate the damage such an expression from Maceo would cause a woman.

'Then I hope it'll tempt you to exit before this vehicle turns into a furnace.'

He alighted, and then, to her surprise, came around to open her door. The teasing smile was widening, triggering a curious mixture of excitement and despair, which intensified the moment she stepped out and inhaled his scent.

Memories of that scent on his hard body plastered passionately against hers immediately took centre stage in her thoughts, then reeled forward through graphic possibilities of what might have happened if they hadn't stopped.

'I've lost you again. Should I be offended? Or flattered?' he asked.

'Flattered?' she echoed hazily.

'Your expression gives you away. But, truly, there's no crime in reliving a unique moment.'

'You must be speaking metaphorically, or something, because I see no crime whatsoever in calling a halt after a foolish decision.'

To her absolute dismay, he smiled with genuine amusement. It utterly transformed his face. A true fallen angel with a wicked streak. His smile promised all sorts of devilish delight. Faye felt her jaw dropping and scrambled to right that wrong.

'We're two level-minded adults, *cara*. With needs that seem programmed to lead us in one direction, whether we wish to go or not,' he rasped, his voice a little rough and a lot disturbing.

'What's that supposed to mean?'

Why on earth was her voice quivering? She wasn't some quaking maiden. She had one experience and its devastating aftermath to her name. And a vow to ensure no more were added to it.

A vow she'd almost broken last night.

A vow she risked now, standing here in the shadow of Maceo's towering frame, getting lost in the accented timbre of his voice and the spellbinding paradise around them.

'It means, whether we like it or not, this thing needs to be addressed.'

Despite his conceited demeanour, there was an edge to the words, indicating that perhaps he wasn't as sanguine about it as he wanted to be.

The hair trigger that demanded she answer with another denial pushed words to the tip of her tongue. Maceo halted them with a simple slide of his forefinger over her lips.

'We really should go inside. I'd hate to see this exquisite skin of yours suffer under this sun.'

As if on cue, a thick drop of sweat slid down her throat and over her clavicle.

His gaze zeroed in on it and Faye felt every inch of the bead's slow trajectory in the rapt expression on his face. Hunger clamoured through her as his nostrils flared. The tip of his tongue glided over his inner bottom lip and Faye experienced it deep in her pelvis, in the hot and needy core of her womanhood.

Move.

She sucked in a desperate breath and dragged her gaze away, only to lose it when his hand slid down her arm to capture hers. Firmly he led her up wide stone steps, through grand oak double doors into a marble-floored foyer with a giant floral centrepiece that gave off sweet perfume through the airy space.

There they were met by a clutch of household staff, who introduced themselves and immediately offered refreshments.

With a cold glass of fruit punch in hand, Maceo shifted into host mode and offered to show her round.

From high-ceilinged rooms with plantation-style shutters that opened out onto exquisite terraces, to a twenty-foot-high pavilion just beyond the main house, fashioned for intimate dining, and a sparkling turquoise pool, every corner of the mansion was breathtaking.

Halfway through the tour Faye kicked off her platform heels, sighing when her feet touched cool stone paving. From a shaded patio, Maceo pointed out the majestic backdrop of the Pitons and the Caribbean Sea. And as her gaze rushed over all that beauty she spotted the sleek yacht moored a quarter of a mile away from the private beach.

It was multi-decked and sizeable, without being overly ostentatious. And yet it sent prickles of awareness skating over her skin. Every space she'd occupied with Maceo so far had offered a sense of freedom—albeit a false one, because Maceo could occupy her space and thoughts even when he was miles away. The yacht, however, seemed...*intimate*.

There was that word again. Creeping far too often and relentlessly into her thoughts.

'Does the inside please you as much as the outside?' Maceo asked when they returned indoors, with that low, deeply disturbing note still in his voice.

Feeling unsettled, she examined his expression for an insight as to the subtle changes in their skirmish. There was no mockery. But there was a quiet, intense emotion she was afraid to decipher.

'It's magnificent,' she answered, simply and truthfully.

He nodded with satisfaction, then straightened from where he'd draped his streamlined body against a wall. '*Bene*. The housekeeper will show you to your room. If you need anything just let the staff know.'

Abruptly he turned away and started to walk off.

'Where are you going?' she blurted.

He paused, then shot her a droll look. 'I'm attempting, perhaps for the first time since we met, to leave while we're not at each other's throats. I think the term is to quit while I'm ahead, *si*?'

Faye was shaking her head before he'd finished. 'Surely we can find a way to coexist and be...?' She stopped, because she couldn't quite find a term that described what not being in conflict with Maceo looked like.

Pleasant? Peaceful? *Affable?*

Words far too tame for the high-octane friction that existed between them.

'Without...?' he pressed, one eyebrow quirked in amusement.

She threw exasperated hands in the air. 'I don't know. But I didn't fly halfway across the world to be left twiddling my thumbs because you're attempting to be...whatever version it is of yourself you're being right now. At the very least can we call a truce on hostilities?'

That smile returned, played at his lips while he stared at her. 'Very well. If that is what you truly wish. Take the remainder of the day. Relax. Work some of the jet lag out of your system. We'll reconvene at some point tomorrow?'

A knot of tension eased inside her and she realised she'd been holding her breath. Because she'd needed that reassurance of when she'd see him again. *Dear God...*

'Sure. Okay.'

With a far too cunning smile, Maceo walked away, leaving her feeling as if she'd walked into another of his silken traps.

The housekeeper arrived to escort her upstairs, relieving her from dwelling on her thoughts. Faye smiled as the older woman informed her with quiet but deep pride that they were in the much sought-after suburb of Soufrière. That she'd worked for the Fiorenti and Caprio families—in her dream job—for over twenty years.

This prompted Faye, just for a moment, to consider asking her about Luigi and Pietro, before dismissing the idea. All she'd be doing was inviting speculation.

In her opulent suite, her clothes had been unpacked and neatly put away in the large dressing room. French windows led onto a sprawling terrace and Faye's breath caught all over again at the magnificent view.

Once the housekeeper had pointed out every luxurious amenity in the bedroom and sky-lit rainforest-themed bathroom, she smilingly enquired about Faye's dinner plans.

Torn between asking about Maceo's plans and remaining oblivious, she settled for a quiet dinner on her terrace. The view was too stunning to waste. And a few hours to get her head straight wouldn't hurt either.

Dinner was a superb seafood salad, washed down with another fruit punch, after which Faye returned to her suite, took off the scarlet linen jumpsuit she'd travelled in and indulged herself for far too long beneath the powerful jets of the shower before sliding between seriously comfortable sheets.

She woke the next day to a message from Maceo that he would be in conference calls all morning and that she had the day to herself.

Faye refused to examine why the message left her hollow inside.

After a lazy breakfast, she powered up her laptop and re-read every report about Casa di Fiorenti's St Lucia operation. Then she fired off an email to Alberto with some new flavour ideas.

Feeling her concentration wavering after that, she gave up, and slipped into a sun-yellow bikini and matching beach dress with a long slit that fell to her ankles.

Barefoot, she went downstairs to the pool. After confirming the time difference, she plucked her phone from her bag. She hadn't spoken to her mother in a few days, and although she wasn't worried about Angela Bishop's well-being, she was suddenly dying to hear her mother's voice.

Her call connected a minute later.

'Hi, Mum? Are you okay?' she asked, when a soft, mellow voice answered.

'Of course I am, Faye. Why wouldn't I be?'

A lump rose in her throat at the clear, lucid response. Her mother was having a good day.

'I'm glad to hear it. What have you been up to?' she asked, reclining on a lounger.

For the next twenty minutes Faye lost herself in her mother's everyday life at New Paths, tossing in a few vague anecdotes of her own. But behind their exchange was the pain and sadness that always lingered.

Faye wasn't aware she was crying until she felt

the wetness on her cheeks. She struggled to pull herself together. The last thing she wanted to do was upset her mother with her silly tears.

She waited for a natural break in the conversation, then ended it with as much enthusiasm as she could muster.

She'd just tossed her phone onto the table beside her when a shadow loomed over her.

'You're distressed. Why?' Maceo demanded tightly.

Faye blinked, struggling to get her emotions under control as he sauntered closer. 'It's nothing.'

'I beg to disagree.'

She pressed her lips together. 'I thought we weren't meeting until later. Why are you here?'

He held out a glass and she realised that he'd come with refreshments.

'It's hot out here. I thought a drink might help,' he stated, his gaze tracking her face. Yesterday's easy humour was nowhere in the eyes that shamelessly dissected her expression.

She accepted the drink while trying to hide the feeling of vulnerability his presence elicited. 'Thank you.'

He claimed the lounger next to hers, his gaze never leaving her face. 'Tell me, or leave me to form several probably wildly inaccurate conclusions,' he said, with a deceptive softness that didn't hide his intent.

Faye dropped her eyes to her glass and then,

fighting weakness, boldly returned his gaze. 'Or you could leave it alone?'

'We seem to have this conversation quite a lot, no?'

'Because you have no qualms about prying, but only deliver information *you* promise when the mood takes you.'

Was this a test? Was getting her to open herself up to him one of the requisites of fulfilling his duty as executor? Or was it something more?

Faye didn't ask, because suddenly she was terrified to find out that his interest was merely a means to an end...

'My mother,' she blurted, then pressed her lips together, stunned by her own response.

'She is unwell?'

She shook her head. 'Far from it. She's in a brilliant mood.'

He frowned. 'And this causes you distress?'

To say any more would be to reveal far too much, so she remained silent.

Of course Maceo wasn't going to be satisfied with that. 'She lives with you on this farm?' he pressed.

'Yes.'

'Perhaps I'm rusty on the mechanics of family relationships, but verifying that she is well and healthy should be a cause for contentment, should it not?'

Faye scrambled to get her emotions under control. 'It is. I am. I'm not even sure why I am crying.'

His tawny gaze turned sceptical.

'Can we change the subject?' she asked, with a touch of desperation.

'Of course. You want to discuss your favourite subject, perhaps?' His silky words held a definite edge.

Faye nodded, uncaring that she was traipsing from one dangerous territory into another.

He remained silent long enough for her to wonder if he'd changed his mind. Then, 'Has it occurred to you that you're searching for answers that are right in front of you?'

'How do you mean?'

His nostrils flared briefly. 'Perhaps Luigi left you for your own good?'

Pain lanced through her, but she pushed past it. 'Would you leave it alone? Without knowing whether your parents loved you or not?'

His face tightened, his jaw clenching for a moment before he released it. Lifting his glass to his lips, he took a large gulp before setting the drink aside. 'I know they cared for me. To the best of their ability.'

'What does *that* mean?'

Jaded, faintly bleak eyes pinned hers. 'Does anyone really love completely? Or is there an inherent selfishness in us that guarantees we'll always hold back? A fear of disappointing others, perhaps?'

'Did you not love Carlotta? Was that not enough?' she asked, plagued by a need to know.

He tensed, his eyes boring deeper into her. 'How

Silence fell between them as his words sank in.

From nowhere, a pulse of potent feminine power flared through her. 'It's just our unique circumstances,' she said.

He shrugged. 'Perhaps.'

One hand moved, tracing the skin where her dress had parted, from mid-thigh to knee, before sliding his hands behind her leg. The sensation was shockingly visceral, enough to draw a gasp.

'If it helps, I don't like it any more than you do.' Before she could respond to that curiously bruising declaration, he continued, 'You think you will forget me that easily, Faye? When you can't even remain within touching distance without your every sense clamouring for me?'

Heat washed through her as his fingers kneaded her flesh. 'I'll take care of how I feel. Feel free to do the same for yourself.'

He didn't respond immediately. Instead his eyes conducted a slow, thorough journey, landing in places that highlighted her breathless state, her helpless reaction to him. She knew her nipples were pebbled against her bikini. That a fine tremble had seized her since he'd laid his hands on her. Her fingers were locked hard into the cushions of the lounger just so she wouldn't reach for him.

'And what way is that? Do be kind and share, *per favore*,' he rasped.

Retreat. Regroup. Anything but sit here, tormented by the need to touch him.

Too late, he saw her struggle. Stoked it.

'Do it,' he encouraged thickly. 'Touch me.'

'No,' she said boldly. Then ruined it by trembling.

That drew a wicked smile from him. And the smile grew the longer she remained seated, weakening her further when he leaned in until his lips were a whisper from hers.

'You're not a coward. Take what you want. Set us both free.'

She drew in a desperate breath, inhaling his potent scent until every pore of her being was filled with him. Slowly his smile disappeared, replaced by a stark hunger that threatened to eat her alive.

How had they got here?

The answer was terrifyingly simple.

They *always* ended up here. As if an invisible force controlled them.

But she wasn't a passive passenger, without any say or control in her destiny. On the contrary, faced with temptation such as she'd never known before, her willpower had pulled her though when things got out of hand.

'We're going to part in a few weeks...'

His words echoed in her head, intensifying the tightness in her chest and the hollow in her belly.

Perhaps it was the need to eradicate those feelings that made her react. Perhaps her foundations had been badly eroded when she wasn't looking.

Whatever.

With a rough, unbidden little sound, torn from

her throat, Faye wrapped her arms around his broad shoulders and closed the gap between them.

Maceo permitted her free rein for all of five seconds, and then he was pulling her into his lap, disposing of the sundress in two easy moves to leave her clad only in her bikini. He reclined on the lounger, dragging her along his body until she was sprawled on top of him. Then he wove dark magic around them.

Words tumbled from his lips as he tasted her with a ferocity that left her breathless. Moaning, she threw herself into the embrace, the knowledge that this exploration was finite, that some time very soon she would be back in Devon with her mother, memories of Capri and St Lucia a distant dream, sharpening the need to absorb and hoard every second of this experience.

She gasped as Maceo flipped them over and dragged urgent hands down her body. Cupping one breast, he flicked the nipple expertly until it peaked, then groaned under his breath. Searing pleasure darted from the point of contact to her core, making her slick and needy and desperate.

Against her thigh she felt his potent power and shivered.

'I want you. I will have you,' he grated against her throat, the sound so raw and deep it was as if he made the oath to himself.

It burrowed deep inside Faye, and the next shiver that coursed through her, while deeply pleasurable, arrived with a warning. Because for a nanosecond every cell in her body had screamed *yes*.

Yes to opening herself up to another devastating rejection.

Yes to putting not just herself and her innocent mother in humiliation's way but Maceo, too.

Because hers was the sort of stigma that could never be washed away.

She'd been selfish once upon a time, had sought solace when she should have kept her secret. She still bore the emotional scars from that.

Matt had only been a fellow university student, but Maceo was Luigi's godson—part of a family her stepfather had treasured and chosen over her mother and her. And, while the knowledge seared pain into her soul, after weeks in his domain she understood why Luigi had made that choice.

Maceo had impeccable pedigree, and despite his tragic circumstances he had become a powerful, dynamic CEO, revered for his intellect. A man who'd elevated his family's business to international renown and success.

How could that compare to her, a nobody, *an abomination*, with a deep, terrible secret?

If she gave in now, even if her secret remained buried for her lifetime, knowing she'd stained him would be unconscionable.

She started to pull away.

He caught her chin and stilled her retreat. The

action left her with very little choice but to stare into intense tawny eyes alight with passion.

'You are thinking of denying me. Denying *us*. *Again*,' he condemned, with a quiet, deadly rasp.

'I… I have to.' The words were torn from her soul.

'The only reason you *have to* is because something holds you back,' he announced arrogantly. His eyes narrowed to laser slits. 'Your HR forms suggested that you are unattached. Is that a lie?'

'You read my HR forms?' she asked, momentarily distracted before his firm touch focused her back on the electric present.

'I'm CEO,' he stated imperiously. 'Now, answer the question. Do you have a lover, Faye?' he breathed, his voice a volcanic rumble as his gaze flicked down to where they were plastered together, chest to chest.

'What? No! If I had a lover I wouldn't even *start*!'

He breathed out slowly. Then, like an approaching tsunami, the hunger in his eyes intensified, growing possessive, blazing with a fire that threatened to turn her every objection to ash.

She knew it was a mistake to keep lying there, feverishly urging her mind to do the right thing when her body was moulded to his.

'*Allora perché?* Why?' he asked throatily, his gaze searching her face as if he would draw the answer from her very skin.

Absurdly afraid that he would achieve that goal, Faye scrambled off the lounger.

'Why?' She repeated his question. 'Here's a question for *you*. Why are you acting as if this is somehow written in the stars? This is not inevitable. Far from it. I don't want you. I don't want *this*.'

The words were flung out with wild, desperate intent—to make them *both* believe it. But all they achieved was drawing Maceo's narrowed gaze, laser beams searching even harder.

'Lie to yourself all you want, *cara*, but don't insult me. We may not be "inevitable", but have you considered that the one way to be rid of this...this *follia* is to get it out of the way?'

She shook her head. *Retreat. Regroup.*

Finally heeding her own advice, she took a few steps back.

Seeing her blatant retreat, Maceo stilled.

They stayed that way, locked in a churning whirlpool of emotions. Every cell in her body screamed at her to close the gap between them once more. Give in to the *follia*—the madness. But how could she while still keeping him in the dark about her secret?

Torn, she turned away. 'I'm going for a swim. In the sea. I may be a while, so you'll have all the time you need to forget this ever happened.'

She snatched up her dress and her bag and hurried away, with every step feeling his eyes boring into her back. She'd nearly reached the stone steps leading down to the beach when his voice stopped her.

'Faye.'

He was close. Far too close.

She didn't look back, terrified in case that face, that body, the heady knowledge that all that determination was focused on having her, swayed her into doing the unthinkable.

'Nothing has changed. I'll see you at dinner. And rest assured that we will visit this subject again. For my own sanity I'll want a better answer than the flimsy ones you have given me so far.'

His words should have been her cue to refuse his dinner plans. To come up with an excuse to stay in her room.

But even that proved impossible. Because on her return she discovered the staff were packing up her luggage.

Her slightly hysterical demand as to why prompted a response in the form of a short, succinct note from Maceo.

Change of plan. We set sail tonight before sunset.

We won't be returning to the villa for a few days.

Maceo

They were visiting the plantations early? Was it because he wanted this trip to be over as soon as possible or because he had another strategy up his sleeve?

The urge to refuse rose again, but only for one futile second. She'd accompanied him of her own free will. Protesting now would be counterintuitive to everything she wanted to achieve. And, while she'd learned a few things about Luigi, one question still needed an answer. Tonight would be the perfect opportunity to demand it.

Besides, wasn't this fractious subject the perfect tool to ensure they didn't stray into dangerous territory? Because when they were discussing Luigi they kept their hands off each other. But then weren't they equally adept at directing every subject back to this impossible attraction between them?

Not tonight, she vowed.

The declaration rang hollow, so she busied herself selecting a dinner outfit before all her belongings were spirited away. Then, with nothing to do but while away the hours, she indulged in a long, luxurious bath.

Inevitably, evening arrived, and she stood on the jetty, waiting to be ferried to the yacht.

She ran nervous fingers over her dress, wondering if she was overdressed. *Too late.* The off-the-shoulder chiffon dress in shimmery ombre colours that progressed from white at the bodice through shades of blue and purple to end in a dark mauve at her feet would just have to do. Besides simple silver hoops in her ears, she'd forgone jewellery, letting her free-flowing hair provide the protective layer—albeit a laughable one—she badly needed.

The seventy-metre yacht was ablaze with golden light, a gorgeous streamlined vessel made more awe-inspiring by its perfect reflection in the glass-smooth water. Each second they grew closer, and Faye's mouth grew drier.

'Nothing has changed...'

'For my own sanity...'

Maceo's words pounded deep and hard inside her until she could hear nothing but his deep rasp, the dark promise in his voice that would surely be her doom unless she employed every self-preservation tactic she could muster.

She was taking calming breaths when the tender drew up alongside the yacht. A steward helped her onboard and led her through stunning reception areas and hallways decorated in gleaming champagne, gold and bronze accents and up several staircases to the main deck.

There, Maceo waited, leaning against the railing with his profile turned away from her as he sipped from a crystal glass. A lightweight sand-coloured suit complemented his pristine white shirt, both colours drawing attention to his vibrant tanned skin and sculpted features.

The steward discreetly melted away, and Faye took a moment to arm herself against the onslaught of sensations Maceo never failed to elicit. She managed two full seconds before his head whipped in her direction, burnished gold eyes zeroing in on her. He searched her face for several seconds, before conducting a slow, tortuous scrutiny of her body.

'*Buona sera*, Faye,' he finally rasped, leaving his position to stride towards her. 'You look sublime.'

'Thank you. I think I read somewhere that yachts and heels don't go together. Do I need to take my shoes off?'

Her question invited extended scrutiny, from her feet to her hair, where it rested for an eternity. 'You may do whatever pleases you,' he murmured silkily, before reaching past her to pluck a fruity concoction that was ready and waiting on a silver tray.

Faye took it from him, sampled it and almost groaned as decadent flavours burst on her tongue.

His lips twitched. 'Good?'

She nodded. 'Very—thank you.'

Maceo nodded towards the railing. 'Come, let's catch the last of the sunset before it's gone.'

Considering his final words to her that afternoon, Faye wondered if this was the first stage in another devious skirmish. But, unlike during his assessment of her, now Maceo's face gave nothing away.

Deciding to accept his invitation at face value, she kicked off her shoes and accompanied him to the railing. The evening would probably turn fraught at some point anyway, on account of the picture tucked away in her clutch bag.

The reminder made her shiver, drawing his sharp gaze.

'Are you cold?'

'No, just… It's nothing.'

Like her, he seemed to accept her response at face value. He started pointing out stunning landmarks to her, and Faye realised the vessel was moving. She cast one last look over her shoulder at the villa, the sense of leaving safety behind dripping apprehension into her veins.

'No need to look so alarmed, *cara*. You will be returned safe and sound.'

'Would you confess if you intended the opposite?' she teased.

Her attempt at humour misfired when his face hardened. 'You have my word that I will always be truthful with you, Faye,' he stated, with such gravity she felt the power of it deep inside.

'Thank you,' she replied, praying he'd lend credence to his words before the evening ended.

After a charged moment he nodded, then slid effortlessly back into host mode. Almost in perfect synchrony, they sipped their drinks as the sun disappeared in a ball of gorgeous flame into the sea.

Then Maceo led her one deck below, to where an elaborate dinner table was set out for two.

The vichyssoise starter was perfect, the poached salmon with grilled sweet potato equally mouthwatering. But what struck Faye most was how much she was enjoying this less intense Maceo. How his infrequent but jaw-dropping smiles curled around her senses, warming that cold, dark place where fear and isolation lived.

She knew it was temporary, that the knot would be back in its rightful place in a few hours. But banishing that warmth was the hardest thing she'd ever done. So she let it linger, lull her into a place of comfort. Just for a little while.

Too soon the plates were cleared, the after-dinner coffee drunk. Nervous over what was coming, she refused Maceo's offer of a nightcap and went with him into another stunning salon, this one partly shielded from the cool night breeze.

He sat down next to her, arms spread over the back of the sofa, his stance deceptively relaxed even though she sensed he was anything but. Hooded eyes speared her.

'There's something on your mind.'

It wasn't a question.

Faye swallowed. 'You said I could trust you to be straightforward with me.'

He tensed, eyes narrowed. *'Si,'* he affirmed.

Trepidation drummed wildly in her belly, but she reached into her clutch bag.

'Good. Here's your chance to prove it.' She held out the picture, aware her hand was shaking, but knowing this felt too big for her to be distracted by that weakness. 'Who is this man?'

CHAPTER EIGHT

AT FIRST HE looked puzzled, and then, deciphering exactly what she held, his hand jerked off the back of the sofa to curl around hers, his features turning dark.

'Where did you get this?' he growled, thunder rumbling in his voice.

Every cell in her body quivered. 'Does it matter? I have it.' She pointed to the third man in the photo. 'And I want to know who this is.'

He dropped her hand as quickly as he'd grasped it. 'Why the curiosity?' he asked, clearly deflecting.

'Why do you think? Because he looks a little like Luigi. Is there a family connection?' she probed when Maceo remained statue-still, his features taking on the formidable look that had terrified her during their first meetings.

But she wasn't terrified any more. He'd lowered his guard in varying degrees since then, shown her enough facets of himself to prove he was human. He hurt and mourned, hungered and smiled, even if in a more elevated realm than most.

She waited him out, watched him rise from the sofa, pace to the railing, his gaze settling heavily into the middle distance.

'*Si,*' he confirmed finally.

She waited for more. One minute. Two.

'That's all you're going to give me?'

Tension gripped his whole frame. He exhaled

slowly before turning to face her. 'Every family has a black sheep. Pietro was the black sheep of the Caprio family. The dark secret no one liked to talk about.'

Faye swallowed. She knew all too well what he meant. She was the dark secret of her own fractured family. Most likely the reason Luigi had left and never returned.

'But who was he to you? To Luigi?'

He shoved his hands deep into his pockets, rocked on his feet once. 'He was Luigi's fraternal twin brother.'

Faye gasped. 'His *twin*?' Her stepfather had had a close sibling and never bothered to tell her?

'Don't be taken in by that. Being twins didn't mean they automatically shared a special bond. *Dio*, they didn't even remotely share personalities. They were as different as night and day.'

'In what ways, specifically?'

Maceo's expression shuttered. But she hadn't come this far to be deterred now.

'Tell me, Maceo. Please,' she pleaded softly.

A faint shudder shook through him and his face softened momentarily before hardening again. 'It is exactly how I have said. You may believe your circumstances to be different, but the Luigi I knew was a fair man, a man of integrity and honour. Whereas Pietro was…not. He was irresponsible and callous and unkind. He drank too much, drove too fast. He did everything to excess.'

'Those are unpalatable characteristics, sure… But that's not why you're reluctant to discuss him. There's more, isn't there?'

He uttered a potent expletive in Italian, his fingers stabbing into his hair. 'I would prefer it if you would leave it, Faye.'

She shook her head. 'We've been dancing around this subject for weeks, Maceo. You give me just what you think is enough to keep me quiet. But it's not enough. It hasn't been from the start. But that's on me. I realise now that I wasn't ready to hear everything. I'm ready now—for better or worse. Please.'

'I'm not unsympathetic. But must we do this tonight?' he pressed, a peculiar note in his voice as his hand drifted to his breast pocket.

About to respond, Faye frowned and looked around. She'd been too nervous earlier, or perhaps too cowardly, to admit it to herself. Now she did. Everything—from the lighting to the dinner setting, the sheer magnificence of the scenery to the soft music piping through invisible speakers— pointed to one thing…

Seduction.

Her eyes darted back to him, to the fire in his eyes. 'Maceo…'

Bleakness tightened his face. With a heavy, resolute sigh, his hand dropped. 'Perhaps you are right,' he announced grimly. 'Let's stop dancing around this. You want it all, *cara*? Well, have the whole sordid feast. Then I will be free of this.'

Was that how he saw her? As an obligation to be dispensed with?

Something moved through her. Profound and seismic. Alerting her that something fundamental was about to change. Perhaps in what he was about to tell her. Perhaps in other ways she was too scared to contemplate.

Faye's fingers twisted in her lap as he prowled forward in that far too masculine and animalistic way to reclaim his seat next to her. He started to reach for her hand. At the last moment he froze, his face tightening as he reversed the action.

Faye's heart sank, her insides hollowing with unnerving alarm. Words of protest rose to her lips, but his next words saved her from disgracing herself.

'Pietro was the snake in what should've been a peaceful paradise. He was the reason I was at odds with my parents in the year before they died.'

The dark pain in his voice was palpable.

'What happened?' she asked.

'For years they knew he was up to no good. But, irrationally, they believed he was redeemable simply because he was Luigi's blood. They gave him chance after chance, including a position at the company—which he shamelessly abused by misappropriating funds until the board voted him off. By the time I was a teenager they'd decided the best way to deal with him was to set him up with a monthly allowance and mitigate whatever damage he caused by paying off the paparazzi and bribing whoever needed quieting to protect the family from disgrace.'

Faye swallowed down her distaste. 'Did that work?'

Bitterness twisted his lips. 'Of course not,' he rasped. 'They'd simply handed him another tool to torment them with. And he exploited it. The drug-taking and drinking worsened. He gambled away a fortune using the Fiorenti name. At one point it seemed all my father and Luigi were doing was retaining lawyers to stop the negative publicity Pietro was landing them with.'

His jaw clenched tight.

'Two months before they died I heard them discussing how to tackle the latest problem. He'd been drinking in a bar in Buenos Aires and got involved in a brawl. One of the brawlers was later the victim of a hit and run.'

Ice slithered down her spine. 'Was it Pietro?'

'He was suspected of it, but there was no concrete proof. The biggest deal Casa di Fiorenti had ever landed was on the brink of being sealed. They couldn't afford even the smallest hint of scandal.'

Faye could guess where the tale was heading. 'So they made it go away?'

'The victim survived and they talked themselves into taking no action because there was no proof, instead of making Pietro face his deplorable ways.

Again. He got off free of blame because he was *famiglia*.' Maceo all but snarled the word. 'Right before my eyes, I was seeing him turn the two men I looked up to into the kind of men who would pay victims of a crime to stay quiet so an irresponsible *idiota* could continue wreaking havoc.'

Clarity brought a sympathetic ache to her heart for what Maceo had suffered, and regret for re-opening old wounds. But she hoped that reliving events he'd probably never discussed before might help him overcome them, maybe even heal in a way she'd never been able to.

'They were your heroes and they let you down. But you're not the sort of man who would just let it go. What did you do?'

'I spent months rowing with my parents over it. The event that night they died wasn't just to cel-ebrate landing the deal. It was also meant to clear the air between us. At least, that's what my mother hoped.'

'But?'

His tawny eyes grew haunted and his lips thinned into a bleak line before he answered. 'But then I discovered that they'd silenced another Pi-etro incident just that morning. So I hurled judge-ment at them. Threatened to remove myself from their so-called *famiglia*. Basically uttered words I never got the chance to take back.'

She placed a hand on his arm, as if it would stop his self-flagellation. 'Maceo—'

'The last thing I said to my father was that I was ashamed to be his son. Those were the words he took to his grave.' He sliced his gaze towards her, his whole body bristling with pain, regret and fury.

She leaned in closer, sliding her hand higher up his shoulder until she encountered the cool skin of his nape. 'I'm sure they weren't.'

He slashed her a mocking look even as he angled his body towards hers. 'You're sure? Because you have personal insight into the afterlife?'

She let the mockery slide. 'Because he'd have to have been a fool not to realise you were speaking from a place of love and concern. And I don't think he was. Sounds like he was just caught in an impossible position.'

He laughed. 'It wasn't impossible. On the contrary, it was very clear-cut to me back then.'

'Why? Because you'd walked in their shoes? Felt the pressure of pouring your heart and soul into a company only to risk it burning into nothing?'

His eyes turned to burnished slits. 'Why, *cara*, you sound like you condone their actions. I take it that means you don't hate Luigi quite as vigorously as you did when you arrived?'

Faye shrugged even as she scrambled to reclaim the foundations of her fortress before the sympathy pouring from her completely eroded it. 'I'm merely trying to help you see things from another angle. You just said *"back then"*. Somewhere deep down you know differently now, don't you?'

He shrugged, but his gaze swept away.

'If you regret judging them, then perhaps you should consider forgiving yourself.'

'Just like that?' he rasped bitterly.

'What's the alternative? Carry this emotional baggage for the rest of your life?'

He swallowed, his hand once again straying to his pocket. 'Yes,' he said finally. But in the shadows of that response she caught a trace of uncertainty.

'Maceo, why do you keep doing that?' She indicated towards the hand on his chest.

He stiffened, his hand bunching before it dropped to his thigh. 'It's nothing I wish to discuss.'

The hollow inside her grew, but she ignored it. 'Can I ask you something else?'

He gave a stiff but regal nod.

'Did Luigi or your father make any provision for Pietro in their wills?'

He frowned, then shook his head. 'No.'

'Doesn't that tell you something? I was nothing to Luigi and he left me potential millions, but he left nothing to his own twin?'

His frown deepened. 'You weren't nothing to him. Clearly you made a huge impact.'

'Did I? Then why didn't he tell me he had a twin brother?'

Bitterness returned full-force. 'For the same reason he tried to suppress Pietro's activities. The obsessive need to keep secrets,' he railed.

Faye stiffened as terrifying reminders of her own secret crashed in. Registering that her hand was still on his nape, she started to withdraw it.

With lightning reflexes Maceo captured it. Eyes on hers, he planted a kiss in her palm, then laid it on his thigh, trapping it there with his hand.

'You know everything now. Every last squalid Fiorenti and Caprio secret. And I thank the heavens for it, because I've grown tremendously bored of the subject,' he drawled thickly.

She forgave the blatant lie so she could fight the disturbing urge to explore the taut, muscled thigh flexing beneath her palm, the male fingers trailing over her wrist and up her bare arm. She shivered when they lingered in the crook of her arm, then watched, terrifyingly fascinated and intensely turned on, as her skin prickled with desire. Even her goosebumps chased after his touch.

'I made a vow years ago, Faye. Sworn over my parents' graves.' He placed a finger over her lips when she opened her mouth to ask what it was. 'It's private. Do you understand?'

She nodded jerkily, her heart racing. Sadly, she understood more than most.

'Your arrival has thrown that vow into chaos. I've decided my only option is to break it. For a while. For my sanity. The consequences be damned.'

Those last words were arrows to her chest. 'No. Maceo, you can't—'

'I can. I will.'

Implacable words forged in steely decision. She knew she couldn't sway him from it.

A curious little sound left her throat as his fingers danced over her left clavicle.

'Yesterday I wanted to taste the sweat that collected right here. For hours afterwards I could think of nothing else.'

The raw, hotly rasped words sucked the breath from her lungs. In an instant treacherous little fires ignited inside her. They stung her nipples into hard, needy points, poured heat between her thighs until she could barely sit still.

Maceo's hand dropped to her waist, dragged her closer, and he caught one earlobe between his teeth. 'From the moment you walked into my office I've been dying to know how long this river of hair runs. Now I know,' he continued in that electrifying monotone, 'and I will wrap it around any limb that takes my whim while I drown in the sweet scent of cherry blossom. And you will let me,' he growled into her ear.

'Will I?' she returned, even as desire pooled in her belly.

'*Basta, arcobaleno. Basta,*' he chided. 'Let's not fight any more. We've exhausted every subject beneath the sun except this one.'

They hadn't tackled one vital subject. *Her.*

Now she knew more of his past, the surer she

was that any connection between them, physical or otherwise, would be an unforgivable mistake.

There was one other subject guaranteed to stop him, and although the feel of his warm lips trailing over her skin nearly stopped her from naming it, she closed her eyes and said, 'Carlotta.'

He stiffened. Against her neck, she heard his harsh breathing.

'I really must commend you for your exceptional ingenuity in summoning these roadblocks, *arcobaleno*,' he breathed as he pulled back.

The pained derision in his voice suggested he was referring to an entirely different sort of blocking.

She shrugged. 'I can't dismiss her.'

He nodded, smoothing a finger almost thoughtfully over her lower lip. '*Bene.* Let's get this over with too.'

He withdrew his touch and she had to clench her belly to stop herself from diving after it.

'I went into that coma as a child. I emerged a man. The company was in serious trouble. Board members were furiously power-grabbing and Carlotta's brothers were intent on seizing my birthright. I couldn't let that happen.' Tawny eyes darkened, inner demons swirling within. 'I faced several months of physical rehabilitation, while she tried to gain firmer ground from where to fight the board. With our shares split under different names we were in a precarious position. It made sense to join forces. We married simply to stop the company from falling into the wrong hands when it became clear that was the only choice.'

'So it was a marriage of convenience?' God, was that *hope* in her voice? Had a part of her not yet accepted the folly of feeling *anything* for Maceo?

He nodded, trailing his knuckles down her cheek. Barely leashed hunger briefly flared to life. 'Exactly so. A platonic marriage that benefited both of us once I was out of rehab.'

She gasped. '*Platonic?* You mean you…you didn't…'

'Share her bed? No, I did not.'

She stared at him, her breath caught in her throat. 'But you were married for almost a decade.'

Piercing eyes hooked into hers. 'If that's your way of asking whether I sought pleasure or release elsewhere, the answer is no,' he said, with the gravity she recognised now.

Faye believed him. From the start he'd seen her as an inconvenience thrust upon him. She wasn't someone he needed to impress or concoct stories for in order to win her over. She was nowhere near the strata he inhabited.

He could have any woman he wanted…

'Why me?' She blurted words she'd had no intention of uttering.

He lounged back against the cushions, eyes burning with that fierce, dangerous light as he gave a low, self-mocking laugh. 'You think I haven't asked myself that same question? There are easier conquests out there than you, *bellissimo arcobaleno*.'

'Then—'

Swiftly, he lunged for her, every trace of humour gone as he threaded his fingers into her hair. 'No, *tesoro*. My patience is exhausted. I won't be indulging you with a lesson in chemistry. Your eyes haven't stopped devouring me since you stepped aboard this boat. You want this, so I can only conclude that you wish me to beg. Is that it? You want me on my knees, pleading for the chance to make you my first?' he growled.

Then he stiffened.

Faye gasped as his final words dripped into her hazy brain. Before she could question him he slanted his mouth across hers in a blinding, possessive kiss, devoured her lips as if he wanted to make her forget what he'd just said.

But despite the glorious sensation of experiencing his kiss she felt his confession throb between them, lending a sharper bliss that came from wondering if this was new to him too. No, he was far too adept at kissing. Far too adept at *everything*.

Just when she feared every cell in her body would fling itself into the cauldron of mounting desire, Maceo eased away. They both struggled for air as he plastered his forehead against hers, his breathing rough and choppy.

'*Santo cielo*, that wasn't how I intended to announce that. Hell, I didn't plan on divulging it at all,' he half snarled.

But he had. And with each passing second the shockwaves intensified.

'How…?' she asked in quiet awe, selfishly seizing another minute to put off confronting her turbulent emotions.

'I discovered very early that my status in life attracted a certain breed of parasites disguised as friends. I was jaded by the time I hit the ripe age of fifteen. Toss in Pietro's unsavoury exploits and their effect on my family and—'

'You didn't want even of a hint of his character associated with you?'

One corner of his mouth twisted. 'I was no saint, *cara*. I might not have performed the ultimate act, but I indulged enough.'

Jealousy spiked her insides. 'Then the accident happened?'

He nodded grimly. 'I was eighteen when it occurred. I didn't emerge from my coma for a year. Through it all Carlotta stayed by my bedside, fighting pressure from doctors and her own brothers to pull the plug. And that was before eighteen months of rehabilitation.'

Fresh sympathy poured through her, and against her better judgement she cupped his jaw. 'Oh, Maceo…'

He kissed her palm. 'Rewarding her with my loyalty and fidelity felt like a small price to pay.'

Honourable words, but she sensed there was more. He was holding something back.

'But it wasn't small. It was a huge sacrifice. Perhaps too big in some respects, even in the name of protecting Carlotta and your family's legacy?'

He tensed again and rose, striding stiffly away from her. 'What do you want me to say? That I didn't feel I had the right to live a happy and comfortable life when my actions had driven my parents and my godfather to their deaths?'

She gasped. 'No! Why would you believe that?'

'Because it's the truth! I was quarrelling with my father, yet again, when he lost control of the car. My words had driven my mother to tears and caused my father to lose concentration. He drove the car off a cliff, resulting in horrific carnage that, by some cosmic twist, I somehow survived. So tell me, Faye, should I have risen from my hospital bed and immediately sought oblivion in a woman's arms?'

His voice was a tableau of raw pain and self-loathing. She jumped up, every cell in her body yearning to reach for him. 'Of course not. But that doesn't mean you can never forgive yourself—'

'I don't deserve forgiveness! I deserve nothing but the misery I have brought upon myself.'

She froze. 'Then why…? *I'm* the reason you're breaking your vow?' she breathed in shock.

He appeared thunderstruck. Then he drove his fingers through his hair, throwing it into sexy disarray. He paced away from her, shoulders heaving as he inhaled, then he charged back, spearing her a narrow-eyed look.

'We've digressed. Yet again.' His tone suggested he was at the end of his rope.

Faye knew she couldn't put it off any longer. 'I want you, Maceo. But I can't have you. And you can't have me.'

A muscle leapt in his cheek. '*Ripeto*. Repeat that.'

'Please—'

He held up a halting hand. 'You plead understanding for something you haven't explained.'

She folded her arms around her middle to stop the cold seeping into her veins from taking hold. 'You're better off not knowing! Please trust me. I don't think your first time should be with someone like me.'

His nostrils flared. 'Why not?'

'Because you'll regret it.'

'That tells me absolutely nothing. Do better.'

'I'm…damaged.'

He turned still as stone and his skin lost colour. 'How?'

She couldn't form the words, so she shook her head.

'No,' he refuted icily. 'You don't get to hold back now. Secrets and subterfuge shattered my family. Whatever it is you believe you're shielding me from, I want it out in the open.'

Ice shrouded her heart. 'You don't. Please, Maceo. I'm not worth it.'

He gave no quarter. 'I will be the judge of that—not you. Tell me.'

She darted her gaze across the deck and beyond, for a wild moment wondering if she could throw herself overboard, swim away until the waters sucked her under. Because surely oblivion would be better than the unshakeable knowledge that she would prove him wrong? That nothing could compare to the repugnant truth she'd guarded so zealously since Matt's heart-wrenching reaction?

'Look at me, Faye.'

Breath shuddering, she met his burning gaze.

'There's no escape from this.'

The sharp edge to his words made her wonder if he meant it literally. Had this been his plan all along? Bring her aboard his magical yacht, set a scene straight from a spellbinding dream and... And what? Show her what she couldn't have?

If so, he'd succeeded. She'd delved beneath the formidable exterior to the heart of the man. And what she'd discovered made her yearn harder for him than before, when this had been purely a physical reaction.

And, because she'd seen him, she owed him the truth buried in her heart.

Her heart dropped to her churning stomach as she forced out words. 'Twenty-six years ago my mother lived in London. She was training to be a nurse, but worked part-time as a waitress. She preferred working the posh parties because they paid better.' Faye dragged her hands up and down her arms to stop the shivering. 'One night she stayed late to clean up and...and one of the male guests attacked her. He...he tied her up, blindfolded her and assaulted her.'

'Mio Dio...' Maceo whispered on a stunned breath, then stepped towards her. 'Faye—'

'No! Let me finish. Please.'

His fists bunched but he nodded.

'The attack was traumatising, and she dropped out of school. Three months later she found out that her rapist hadn't just taken from her. He'd left her with a permanent reminder.'

She forced herself to meet Maceo's gaze. She knew what was coming and she refused to hide from it.

'He left her pregnant. With me.'

Maceo's face drained of all colour as a wave of visible shock washed over him. Before it could take full hold, before the accompanying horror, disgust and, worst of all, that nanosecond of weighing up which way to go—whether it was worth bluffing his way through his revulsion or fully revealing it—she turned and fled.

'Faye!'

His voice was a firm command she didn't intend to heed. Absurdly thankful that she'd discarded her shoes earlier, she flew down the stairs. From their tour, she remembered the staterooms were on the lower deck and made a mad dash for them, desperate to put a solid locked door between her and Maceo.

Halfway down the carpeted hallway she lunged for a familiar-looking door, her heart banging against her ribs when she heard his footsteps behind her.

Safely inside, she turned to bolt the door.

One long arm thwarted her, followed by his large, immoveable frame as he filled the doorway. Faye chose the safer option of backing away from him. Of looking anywhere but into a face no doubt filled with horror and revulsion.

She sucked in a desperate breath when the tips of his polished shoes appeared in her lowered eyeline.

'Faye. *Cara*—'

She jerked away from the hand rising towards her. 'Don't touch me. I don't want you here. I don't want your pity. Or your morbid curiosity. Or whatever this is!'

His hand dropped. 'Explain to me why I am the focus of your anger,' he invited, with a quiet calm that perversely ignited her anger. Anger that made her forget she wasn't intending to look into his face. Into eyes that stared back at her with stomach-hollowing ferocity.

'Because I warned you and you didn't listen!'

His head tilted with mocking arrogance. Then he had the audacity to nod in agreement. 'True. You warned me that you were *"damaged".* He had the gall to use air quotes. 'That I would "regret it". Oh, and something about you not being worth it. Have I got everything?'

'No!' she railed. 'You haven't adequately described your disgust. The horror I saw on your face!'

Mockery and arrogance fled and his face assumed the formidable façade that made lesser men quake in his presence. 'Of course I'm horrified. No woman should have to endure what your mother went through.'

'You…' She stopped. Sucked in a stunned breath as his words sank in.

'Any man who harms a hair on a woman's head isn't worthy of the name. Any *bastardo* who does what was done to your mother is a deplorable waste of space who deserves to be thrown into the darkest pit,' he condemned, flames roaring in his eyes.

Faye shook her head, unable to comprehend his reaction.

'As for what you believe should be my reaction to *you*…' He dragged a hand over his jaw, bewilderment flitting over his face. 'Why would you expect me to blame you for something you had no control over?'

Old flames of humiliation and shame washed over her. 'It's never stopped most people in the past.'

'Who?' he snarled.

Her heart twisted. 'Someone I was involved with…briefly. He called me an abomination.' Among many other things.

His nostrils flared. 'Then he too was a despicable idiot. And I believe I warned you before that I'm not *most people*.'

She wanted to laugh hysterically. Of all the times to remind her he was extraordinary!

Her insides rumbled, as if the tectonic plates formed of every negative emotion she'd suffered because of the circumstances of her birth were attempting to shift. Simply on the strength of his words?

'Why are you trying to convince me that this isn't… That you're not…?' *Completely and utterly nauseated by me?*

He sighed. 'It seems that, like me, you need re-educating, *cara*.' His voice was firm, yet gentle.

The rumbling intensified. Faye shut her eyes and tried to calm the roiling. When she opened them he was closer. *Much* closer. Breath-robbing gravity pinned her in place.

'No child should have to bear the burden of the circumstances of their birth,' he said. 'Or permit those circumstances to get in the way of what they want.'

Her head spun. She felt turned inside out. She'd been convinced this would go so differently. And now…

Now she needed a moment—*several* moments—to think.

'Can you leave, please? I'd like to be alone.'

'I'm afraid I can't oblige you, seeing as you are in *my* bedroom, *mio dolce*,' he drawled.

Heart leaping into her throat, she spun around.

Sure enough, she was confronted with unapologetic masculinity. Masterful decoration and effortless sophistication created by a man who knew what he wanted and expressed it in his surroundings. Bold greys blended with dark bronze highlights. There were sharply angled shapes and edgier art than she'd seen in any of the Fiorenti properties so far, displayed on the walls and cabinetry. But the massive bed she'd somehow missed when she'd stumbled into the room was what really gripped her attention.

As she stared at it, dumbfounded, the atmosphere in the room shifted. Morphed and thickened with a different vibe that catapulted her blood through her veins at triple speed. She didn't need to turn to know he was watching her. She knew the instant he started towards her. Because a raw and primitive drumbeat started at her core and spread like brush fire through her.

She heard the rustle of clothes and pivoted to find him tugging off his jacket. With casual ease, he tossed it over a nearby seat.

'What are you doing?'

'Making myself comfortable.'

He kicked off his shoes, then walked past her to the bedside table, where he slid off his sleek wristwatch and set it down.

Somehow those small, intimate, everyday actions were enough to set off several more blazes inside her. She stood there, mesmerised, as he slowly strode past her, positioned himself behind her and cupped one shoulder with his hand. The other lazily threaded through her hair, caressing, shifting, until to her breathless astonishment it was suddenly a loose rope, wrapped around his wrist. Only then did he lean in closer, align his head with hers so his lips brushed her ear.

'*"I want you, Maceo."* Your words,' he reminded her thickly.

His heat engulfed her. 'There were other words too.'

'*Si*, spoken when you laboured under a misapprehension,' he pointed out. 'One that made the gross error of assuming I would choose anyone less than an exceptional woman to experience this with.'

Faye's core melted, reshaped itself into a form she wasn't quite prepared to examine. Not when her every sense was fully under his control, a raw lump of willing clay, yearning to be moulded into any shape he desired.

'Do you believe I'm that woman?' she asked. She needed to know. To be absolutely sure.

He hesitated for one heart-rending moment. Then, 'In this moment, when you're all I can think about, taste, smell, *crave*? *Si...*' he responded thickly, gently tugging the rein he'd made of her hair, exposing her neck to the thrill of his wandering lips.

The drugging desire that swelled through her was almost enough to make her disregard his words.

Almost.

But *'in this moment'* lingered—a tiny but unmissable blemish for a person who'd lived her life intimately familiar with stains. And on top of that he'd made a vow…one whose full details she didn't know but could guess. Both were searing reminders that this thing had a very limited shelf life.

She twisted in his arms with a whimper, to confront her desire full-on.

He tilted her head back, stared deep into her eyes. 'Tell me you want this, *mio dolce*,' he breathed.

'I want this,' she whispered, urgency powering through her.

He didn't waste another second before he slammed her body into his.

Several salacious facts buffeted her at once. She was doing this—truly experiencing a sexual encounter without shame or secrets for the first time in her life. He wasn't repulsed by her. He'd chosen *her*. No matter how temporarily, Maceo wanted her with a fever that blazed in his eyes.

His hand trailed over her hip to flatten in the small of her back. He tugged her closer until she felt the bold imprint of his manhood. She gasped, tried to pull back when she registered his impressive size. He kept her prisoner in the circle of his arms, his eyes raking her face.

'Stay. Feel what you do to me,' he urged, his voice gritty with rough desire.

Feminine power ploughed through her. With almost unnerving abandon she rose on her bare tip-toes and pressed her breasts into his chest.

He shuddered, and then he was kissing her with the kind of savage hunger that powered those tectonic plates inside her, shifted the centre of her axis just that little bit more. And yet it warned her there would be ripples long into her future. Long after she'd left this...*him*...behind.

Faye suppressed the thought. Moaned as his tongue curled around hers. Trembled when his teeth nipped at her bottom lip in a carnal sampling that left her reeling. She might have one experience to her name, but Maceo was the true connoisseur. Within minutes she clung to him, every sinew weak with need.

One strong arm banded her waist and lifted her off her feet. Long strides placed them in front of the bed. Slowly he slid her down his front, hissing out a breath when her softness moulded against him.

He raised her arms above her head, caught them in one hand and held them there, in preparation for their own unique dance. His gaze fused with hers; he slowly tugged at her zip and her dress fell to her waist. A firm push and the soft material pooled at her ankles, leaving her in only tiny lace panties.

Without breaking their locked gaze, he linked their hands, palm to palm. '*Mio Dio*, but I'm going to take my time with you,' he vowed, in a gravel-rough voice.

And she was going to expire—she was certain of it.

He kissed her. Surprisingly softly considering the passion that bristled from him. Heart-stopping. Poignant.

Faye felt tears prickle at her eyes. He pulled away again and she sucked in a shaky breath as he spun her around to face the bed. Slowly, excruciatingly, he traced the outline of her body from wrists to thighs. Then he followed the caress with his lips, down the column of her spine.

'Il mio bellissimo arcobaleno,' he rasped against her skin. My beautiful rainbow.

Faye felt beautiful. Almost…*treasured.*

She knew she was getting carried away, but she couldn't help it.

When he placed one hand in the small of her back and nudged her, she teetered forward onto her hands. Firm hands removed her panties, feathered caresses up the inside of her thighs. Before she could draw breath Maceo parted her in the most elemental way, tasting her with a voracious kiss that weakened every atom in her body.

'Oh, God!'

Shocked pleasure sizzled up her spine as her night of firsts continued. His tongue wrung bliss from her, and when she climaxed he was there to catch her. To hold her close as he drew back the sheets and placed her in the middle of the bed.

Then he made her wait as he finished undressing. A man fully comfortable in his own skin, he stood tall and proud, content to stare down at her with savage hunger while she fought the urge to squirm with the renewed need flaying her.

Slowly he prowled onto the bed, positioned himself over her so she was caged in his arms. He kissed her in slow, languorous strokes, as if he had all the time in the world.

'I feel the need to make you come again,' he delivered hoarsely.

'Because you like seeing me lose control?'

'Because it's the most beautiful thing I've ever seen,' he growled, then flicked his tongue over one nipple.

Need clamouring through her, she arched her back, presented her other breast and revelled in his unfettered shudder as he accepted her offer.

He teased and tormented her. And just when she imagined she'd go out of her mind he reached for a condom. After sliding it on, he grasped her knees.

'Show me where I crave to be, Faye,' he pleaded gruffly.

Knowing she had him under her spell, even if only for a brief time, filled Faye with a heady power and worthiness she'd never experienced in her life. Every ounce of self-consciousness evaporated as, watching his rapt, breathtaking face, she parted her thighs.

Maceo inhaled long and deep, hectic colour scouring his cheekbones as he stared at her feminine core. Then his fingers slowly brushed her flesh. '*Dio mio*, you're so soft,' he rasped thickly.

Faye reached for him, unable to stem her need. 'I want you *now*, Maceo.'

He parted her wider, settled between her thighs. 'Then tell me you're ready, *tesoro*.'

'I'm ready,' she whispered.

In one smooth thrust, he slid into her.

Maceo felt as if his heart would beat right out of his chest. He'd stepped off the path he'd designated for himself, a path that already burned beneath his feet, because of the woman beneath him. Her scent. Her smile. Her very *uniqueness*. In that moment, embedded deep within her, he was sure he could search the whole world and never find another close to Faye Bishop.

But he didn't need to. The woman who quieted his demons was right here. Her tightness was welcoming him in ways he'd only dreamed about. Now he understood why men went to war over sex.

He bit back a groan as she gripped him tighter. As she squirmed.

'Please, Maceo,' she begged.

His vision hazed. He fought for control, noting the tremors shaking the fingers he used to smooth back her hair. He traced her brows, her cheekbones, her nose and the bottom curve of her trembling mouth.

'Hush, *bella arcobaleno*. I've waited a long time for this. Allow me a moment to savour it.'

She stilled, her eyes glazing with a look he wanted to distil and devour on a daily basis. Long after they'd parted ways. Long after this moment of madness had passed and he had recommitted himself to his vow.

Exhaling, he stole another minute. But soon the sensation got too much. He moved. Then groaned as sublime pleasure pulsed though him. The pure magnificence of it merely evidenced why he didn't deserve it.

'That doesn't mean you can never forgive your-self...'

He pushed her tempting words away. Concentrated on her.

She squirmed again, making his breath catch. '*Santo cielo*, you're exquisite.'

Words fell from his lips as he stroked in and out of her. Perhaps this transcendent moment was exactly what he was meant to experience? So he could truly appreciate it and make amends? For how could he suffer if he didn't truly know?

Maceo thought a lot of things as the woman beneath him cried out in release. As soul-stirring pleasure overtook him. Most of all he thought about how bleak his life would be after this. And wondered how the hell he was going to survive it.

But perhaps he didn't need to?

CHAPTER NINE

HE REMAINED AWAKE long after Faye fell asleep, treacherous thoughts weaving through his mind. With a few defiant sentences she'd struck a match that now blazed high, illuminating the dark spaces of his beliefs. The girl with the rainbow hair had offered a different perspective he'd refused to consider before.

Marriage and family were still out of the question. But perhaps he didn't need to remain trapped in the shadows with his guilt and regret. Maybe he'd been spared for a reason...

Dared he reach for it?

No. Because the kernel of alarm he'd experienced when she'd shown him Pietro's picture had only been diminished because of the enthralling experience that had followed. In the aftermath its drumbeat grew again, demanding attention.

He pulled Faye closer, running his fingers through her hair. Her serene post-coital expression drew a very male, satisfied smile from him. The experience had shattered him, and he was certain it had shattered her too. And as much as desire was already reawakening, urging him to relive the event *immediately*, Maceo denied the need.

The subject looming at the back of his mind couldn't be ignored. But that didn't mean he wanted to dissect it with Faye.

Too much had happened tonight. He wasn't

ashamed to admit he needed a reprieve. Reprieve in the form of sex would be ideal but, glancing down at the sleeping woman in his arms, he knew he needed a different avenue.

With a sigh of regret, he slowly extricated himself from her. Her murmured protest prompted a smile, which disappeared as he headed into his bathroom.

Powerful jets cleansed his body, but they did nothing to allay the growing certainty that Luigi hadn't married Faye Bishop's mother under normal circumstances. The connections were too strong to deny, and the possible reasoning behind Luigi's first marriage very much pointed to the actions he knew his godfather would have taken.

More secrets in the name of protecting the *famiglia*.

More covering up of the misdeeds of Pietro Caprio.

But even as Maceo's suspicions hardened he couldn't help but speculate—with the benefit of Faye's own words in his head now—if there hadn't been a best-case scenario behind the act. Whether Luigi hadn't acted with the well-being of his family at heart.

For the first time since his teenage years Maceo could almost accept that explanation without rancour.

The woman in your bed did this for you.

There was no mistaking Carlotta's voice in his head, prompting him down another path. Had this been her intention all along? For Faye to throw doubt on his goals? And what of him? What was *he* supposed to do for her besides hand over her inheritance and the letter that still burned a hole in his desk drawer? A letter that might well answer a few of his own questions, never mind hers?

Regardless of Carlotta's expectations, Faye in his bed was a delightful bonus, and the thought triggered a predictable reaction in his body—one he welcomed simply because it stopped him thinking of Luigi and Pietro. Of their possible connections to Faye.

Tomorrow. The day after. Perhaps even next week would be time enough to chase the answers he sought.

Aware he was hiding, taking the easy way out, he straightened abruptly from where he'd leaned against the tiles.

And then, like a breathtaking rainbow emerging from the stormy clouds of his thoughts, Faye appeared in front of the fogged shower screen. She looked a touch tentative, then she smiled.

During their encounter in bed he'd surprised a few expressions on her face—enough to convince him that while he might be marking his first true experience, she was almost equally unschooled. The thought triggered a primitive pulse of satisfaction. Against every better judgement, he reached out and drew her into the shower.

Her gaze swept hesitantly over his face before

meeting his. 'Are you sure you want me in here? You looked as if you had the weight of the world on your shoulders just then.'

He slid his hands over her silky skin and cupped her delicious bottom, allowing himself the reprieve of completely pushing the subject of Pietro to the back of his mind. 'Not the whole world, *cara*. Just one small dilemma.'

'Which is…?'

She slid her arms around his neck and he bit back a hiss at the effect of her nipples grazing his chest.

'I was debating how long I should allow you to sleep before waking you.'

'Then it's a good thing I only needed a ten-minute power nap.'

Maceo felt his smile widening. Even that strange lightening in his heart didn't surprise him. He'd experienced sublime physical intimacy for the first time in his life tonight. On top of myriad shocking revelations. What was one more ground-shaking reaction?

'Is that a challenge to my manhood?'

She reared back. 'What?'

'That sounded suspiciously like a complaint for not adequately wearing you out.'

She blushed and, *Dio mio*, he wanted to taste every shade of it.

'If that's the case you only have to say the word if you want more.'

Her delicate nostrils quivered, but her gaze was bold as she stared into his eyes. 'I want more, Maceo.'

What are you doing?

He sealed her in his arms, ignored the inner harsh, demanding query and gave her more.

Until he shattered from head to toe once again.

Until her cries filled his ears and warmed parts of him he'd been convinced would remain stone-cold for ever.

Until the only thought that remained in his head as he carried her back to bed was how quickly he could seek oblivion in her arms again.

He continued to ignore that inner voice and they continued to shatter one another in the sun-filled days that followed.

Unsurprisingly, Faye had quickly gathered a clutch of admirers when they'd arrived at the first plantation. Her genuine, almost childlike enthusiasm, her capacity to learn and her unabashed interest in every facet of the production that went into a Casa di Fiorenti confectionery box endeared her to his employees instantly.

Like Pico's slavish devotion, her fan base only grew with each subsequent encounter and now, on their sixth and last day in St Lucia, he watched from his vantage point on his private beach as she charmed the employees he'd invited to a Caribbean-style barbecue.

Despite the intoxicating reggae beats that epitomised the party mood, Maceo remained...*off.* He wasn't in the mood to search for the reason behind his disgruntlement. But, deep inside, he knew the irritant had something to do with the woman who flitted from group to group—barefoot, of course—wearing another concoction of bright clothes that made her blend in perfectly with her exotic surroundings.

At this precise moment she was chasing after the exuberant child of an employee, her unfettered rainbow hair arcing behind her. She disappeared behind a palm leaf cabana, and Maceo dropped his gaze to stare broodingly into his rum punch.

Enough with this cat and mouse game. Until recently he'd been a man who didn't shy away from challenges. A man who stuck to his vows. Yet here he was, evading emails from his R&D director.

It turned out that, while they'd been exploring St Lucia, Faye had been collating ideas for new products and sending daily reports to Alberto Triento. The man was rapturous over the quality of work Faye had produced. Enough for him to question why Maceo hadn't offered her a permanent position at Casa di Fiorenti.

What irked Maceo was that he'd contemplated that very idea. Faye had a degree in business, after all. And her social skills were exemplary. So why was she wasting away on a farm?

Which brought him to his next problem...

The discreet investigation he'd initiated the morning after their first night together had already borne fruit. Most of which, while not conclusive, pointed in the direction he'd hoped they wouldn't.

He tightened his jaw as his demons howled.

More secrets.

He sucked in a grim breath. Faye should be told, of course. But what if it was all a huge coincidence? What if Luigi *hadn't* gone to England purposely to seek out Faye's mother? What if—

His gut tightened as soft, warm fingers slid over his nape. Inhaling sharply at the pulse of pleasure that burst to life inside him, he glanced up.

Faye stepped in front of him, another hesitant smile playing at her lips. 'Any reason why you're so grumpy at your own party?'

'Perhaps because I don't like parties?'

She tilted her head, her long hair swinging over one shoulder. 'And yet you keep throwing them…' she mused.

He shrugged, not quite seeing the point in divulging that *she* was the reason he was throwing this one in particular, after overhearing her express sadness that she wouldn't see the plantation workers and their families again. Why her mournful expression had triggered him into having his privacy disrupted for the better part of an afternoon he chose to ignore, in favour of pulling her into his lap.

She came with a willingness that smothered a layer of his disgruntlement. And when she leaned into him he refused to name the sensation powering through him. Although it closely resembled... *elation.*

'It's our last day on the island. I thought it appropriate to mark it in some way,' he said.

'There are many ways to celebrate. You picked one that involved all your employees. Are you trying to hide the fact that you *like* to give back?'

He lowered his head until their foreheads touched. 'Give me an hour or two and I'll show you just how much I can give back,' he suggested gruffly.

She laughed, and the sound transmitted itself straight through his blood into his chest.

She started to rise. His grip tightened on her convulsively.

'Maceo...?'

Thoughts crowded his head—the uppermost one being the fact that he needed to come clean. About his suspicions over Luigi and Pietro. About his investigations. About the letter.

But until he was absolutely certain, why risk causing her hurt by raking open old wounds? Why alarm her unnecessarily if all this turned out to be false?

'Go. Enjoy yourself. But be warned that I intend to throw everyone off the beach in an hour. I wish to be alone with you.'

She blushed, and another pulse of pleasure unravelled inside him. She was truly a sublime novelty. Enough for him to silently extend himself a little more time to explore the uniqueness of it all.

'Okay. I'll go and warn them, so they're not completely horrified when it happens.'

'*Grande*. Go,' he instructed, then countered his command by pulling her close and slanting his mouth over hers.

Maceo didn't care who saw. She was his. For now. Until he did his duty.

Her soft moan brought that peculiar lightness to his chest once more. He tugged her closer, kissed her with a boldness that announced to every male in the vicinity that she was his. When he was thoroughly satisfied that he'd made his point, he released her.

She scrambled away from him with a dazed look. In that moment, temporarily satisfied with his world, and the knowledge that whatever his report brought he would deal with it adequately, Maceo raised his glass to his lips and drained the punch.

'You're brooding again.'

Faye immediately hated herself for blurting out the observation. It wasn't as if Maceo was ever overly talkative. But she couldn't ignore the fact that he'd grown increasingly laconic over the last few days, prompting her need to discover why earlier at the party.

She'd walked away with no answers, just a kiss

that had left her insides shivery. Hours later, she was no further enlightened.

Was he bored already? Had their chemistry fizzled out so soon for him?

The dismay thickening in her gut didn't shock her. She'd sensed this coming, but foolishly buried her head in the sand.

'Tell me about New Paths,' he said abruptly. 'How long has your mother been there?'

She froze as tiny ice droplets slid down her spine. 'Why?'

His stare was level. Almost neutral. 'You think I shouldn't be curious about where you come from?'

'Um…no, I guess not.' She tamped down her nerves. 'What do you want to know?'

Their conversation over the past few days had been thrilling and engaging. The kind that effortlessly went on long into the night and kept her rapt, to the extent that she feared how attached she'd become to the time she spent with him.

And that was before their lovemaking. Just thinking about *that* drove sensations through her being she couldn't comprehend. Faye understood the basics of chemistry, but *this* was entirely unfathomable to her. Had Maceo not confessed his uninitiated status she would never have believed it. From that very first time he'd leapt into another stratosphere. To say he was insatiable was an understatement.

Their second day onboard the yacht he'd pulled

her into his arms right on the top deck and calmly freed her from her bikini. Her shocked laughter had elicited a dark chuckle in response, followed by, 'I have more than a decade of sex to make up for. And you, *dolce bellissimma*, are so very responsive. How can I not have you like this?'

Every touch, every kiss, every wicked look from his flame-filled eyes surged through her, taking her from one peak to another.

'Am I losing you?' he murmured now, a knowing tone in his voice.

Heat crept up her neck as she recalled that, while their conversation had skirted the outside edge of personal, it had never strayed this close to her past.

'Mum's been at New Paths for over twelve years.'

'So you grew up there with her?'

She shook her head. 'I only spent school holidays with her. The rest of the time I was away at boarding school.'

His eyebrows rose. 'Boarding school?'

'Yes. The school I attended had a special programme. Every year they picked five students to attend a top boarding school. I was lucky enough to get a place.'

'Perhaps luck had nothing to do with it,' he murmured, that pensive look in his eyes again.

'What do you mean?'

He shrugged. 'Your intelligence is exceptional. I'm willing to bet that alone earned you a place.'

Faye wasn't sure why the compliment didn't

quite hit the sweet spot. Why it made the back of her neck tingle.

In the next moment he relaxed in his seat again. 'Alberto has been singing your praises.'

Her heart leapt with delight, her befuddlement fading. 'Really? He's been alarmingly quiet about the emails I sent him.'

'To me, he's been positively exuberant,' Maceo retorted drily.

Delight ballooned and she laughed. 'Sneaky man.'

'Si...' Maceo responded indulgently. He set down his glass, his eyes resting on her with that intensity that made her aware of every inch of her body. 'He even suggested I should give you a permanent position in the company.'

Her insides somersaulted in a mixture of alarm and something else she wasn't ready to name. 'I... Why would he do that?'

He shrugged. 'Your contribution has made an impact. Perhaps he sees an asset that will benefit the company.'

Asset. Benefit.

Being discussed in such cold business terms should put her off. And yet... 'And you? Do you concur?' she asked, despite her glaring recognition that the question bordered on the personal zone.

Having sex with him because she wanted to was one thing. Casually inviting him to give a verdict on her worthiness to his business, when her future couldn't include him, was an open invitation to pain and misery.

It terrified her enough to say, 'You don't need to answer that.'

'I don't? Why not?' he invited.

His eyes bored into her, as if trying to divine her thoughts.

'Because I'm leaving in a few weeks.'

'And if I took Alberto Triento's advice and offered you a job? What would you do, Faye?' he queried softly, in direct opposition to the fire burning in his eyes.

Faye was stunned by how much she wanted to say yes. To rearrange every silly dream she'd harboured for the sake of remaining by this man's side for a little longer.

The power of it robbed her of breath, before she forced common sense in. 'I'd say don't let him influence you into making a hasty decision.'

Several seconds passed as he stared at her, his eyes darkening several shades. The brief flaring of his nostrils signalled his displeasure, but in the next moment he shrugged.

'Perhaps you're right. I shouldn't rearrange my life for a novelty.'

The words stung, as they were meant to, reminding her of other words.

'I made a vow...'

He'd said those words just a handful of days ago. She'd blinded herself to them, and to the contemplative looks he'd slanted her way since, when he thought she wasn't paying attention.

Faye fiddled with her water glass, growing anguish twisting her insides.

She started when he abruptly rose from the dinner table beneath the pavilion in the villa. Tonight he wore dark trousers, paired with a midnight-blue linen shirt that did wonderful things for his olive complexion. Two strides and he was before her. Her body clenched in anticipation as she stared into his eyes, acknowledged the ferocious passion etched into his face.

When he grasped her elbows and tugged her up, she rose to join him. There was a sizzling edge to his passion that intensified his lovemaking, she'd discovered to her delight and dismay, and she was very partial to it.

'You've spent the day charming my employees. Now I think it's time for you to shower *me* with your attention.'

He swung her into his arms and strode away from the pavilion, through the villa—mercifully devoid of staff—and up the grand staircase into his suite. There, he took his time to slide her down his body, ensuring she felt her full effect on him.

Before her feet had fully touched the floor he was winding her long hair around his wrist, a practice he'd grown rabidly attached to. The act triggered an equally visceral reaction within her, and before the coil of hair was fully wrapped around his wrist her core had shamelessly dampened, throbbing with a needy drumbeat that made her breathless.

Maceo didn't kiss her immediately. He simply examined her with quiet intensity. Gripped by an urge she couldn't fathom, she hooked her fingers into the space at the top of his open-necked shirt and pulled it apart.

'Santo cielo!,' he swore under his breath, his nose flaring with wicked arousal, right before he lowered his head and bit her bottom lip. 'More,' he demanded gruffly.

She kissed his throat, trailed caresses down his sculpted chest, and then, growing bolder, nipped his firm skin. His breath hissed and he shuddered.

'More?'

'Si...' he growled thickly.

Faye lost all sense of time and self. She devoured him as if it was their last time. As if he was the last meal she would ever consume. Something had happened during their conversation and it had slid a layer of edgy unease between them. She couldn't pinpoint the cause, yet she felt it. It fed her urgency, and when Maceo stumbled back against the wall she fell on him, a ravenous creature she didn't recognise.

Thick, provocative words fell from his lips as her eager hands undressed him. When he was completely naked, a virile god arrogantly demanding worship, she fell to her knees. A glance up showed his rapt, savage expression.

Vibrating with feminine power, she took him in her hand and wrapped her lips around him. A tortured groan rumbled from his throat, fuelling the fire of her passion. With her tongue and her lips and her hands she feasted on him until his knees buckled. Until he pulled away with a tortured, *'Basta, per favore.'*

One hand urged her up. The moment she stood he reversed their positions and pinned her against the wall, a formidable, virile male in control. One thick arm wrapped around her waist, he settled himself between her thighs, his eyes fixed heatedly on hers, and thrust into her.

Her primal scream bounced off the bedroom walls. It was followed by a series of needy cries, which he answered with overwhelming vigour. Locked together, they feasted on each other until sweat slicked their skin, until their breaths were fused into one life sustaining stream, until it all culminated in a mind-melting release that shook her very soul.

Maceo followed swiftly behind, his powerful body shuddering in her arms as he let go.

She was still floating when he carried her to his bed, when he slid them both between the sheets and pulled her close. But, as much as she wished for oblivion, Faye found herself awake long after his breath had evened out in deep sleep.

Her eyes darted in the darkness as she struggled to rationalise what was happening.

Dismay deepened as the answers she'd held at bay smashed through her barriers.

Everything that had happened between them from the moment she'd arrived in Italy was beginning to make a devastating sort of sense. This was never going to be an emotionless interlude. Even without the sex, Maceo had affected her on a deep, visceral level.

Gradually, that irritating little niggle she'd felt at the dinner table unveiled itself.

She didn't want to leave Italy. Not just yet. And it had nothing to do with her stepfather or Carlotta or anything she'd learned so far.

She wanted to stay because of Maceo.

The thought terrified her more than anything had terrified her in a long time. And yet still she stayed in his arms. And when he woke an hour later and slanted her that brooding look in the dark she melted straight into him.

Because her foolish heart didn't know any better.

Ghana was sublime. A sprawling metropolis in parts. A verdant jungle paradise within half an hour of leaving the capital, Accra. Sitting just above the equator, it was humid during the day and cool in the evening. But what took Faye's breath away was the sudden majesty of its thunderstorms. They arrived with tremendous force, shook the world and drenched everything in sight within seconds.

From her vantage point in the world's most spectacular tree house, in the middle of the Ashanti Region's jungle, she marvelled at the green lushness around her. Everywhere she looked cocoa trees swayed with gentle grandeur for miles, in the rich landscape she'd explored twice over since their arrival two days ago.

Faye had learned every little thing about the precious cocoa bean—especially the new variety of rose-pink bean that was setting the confectionery world alight. But, more than that, she'd collected samples of the indigenous fruits of Ghana and intended to add them to Alberto's collection.

Thoughts of returning to Naples brought apprehension. Somewhere between St Lucia and Ghana, Faye had talked herself into letting this thing ride out in its own time. It might end tomorrow. It might end the day she left Italy. The only certainty was that it *would* end.

Maceo hadn't mentioned the job offer again. And, as much as she told herself she was fine with that, her chest tightened every time she contemplated her inevitable departure.

In other ways, her emotions had been soothed. Maceo's insistence on Luigi's integrity had left her with the belief that her stepfather hadn't forgotten about her. She only wished he'd found time to explain his desertion in the years before his death.

But dwelling in the past was futile. She didn't begrudge him the happiness he'd found.

Would she find a love like that some day?

Her heart lurched when her thoughts immediately zeroed in one specific figure. A strong, formidable Italian who, as if she'd summoned him by thought alone, now slid his arms around her waist.

To disguise his effect on her, and to stop herself thinking that in mere weeks she would leave and possibly never see him again, she jerked her chin at the spectacular theatre of the raging storm. 'I've never seen anything like it.'

'*Si*, it's magnificent, isn't it?'

'The foreman, Kojo, says it can last several weeks.'

Maceo's chin nudged the top of her head. 'It's why I prefer to come at this time. If I had to choose between thunderstorms and the mosquitoes in the latter months of the year, I'd choose this.'

Faye smiled, even though she remained a mess inside. 'Are you saying you're afraid of a few mosquitoes?'

His lips twisted in a half-smile. 'I prefer to battle opponents that don't sneak up on me in their attacks,' he said.

Before she could respond his arms dropped, and he walked back into the tree house.

Made up of two large, opulent rooms, divided into living and sleeping areas, it was built into the branches of a giant wawa tree, with the actual walls of the tree house made of the same wood. Locally made rugs covered the floors and walls, and an embroidered throw with a cocoa theme covered the king-sized bed. Off the side of the bedroom was a rainforest shower and bathroom, and adjoining the living room an alcove with a large desk that Maceo had commandeered.

Faye watched him go, rubbing her arms to stop the cold shiver that had nothing to do with the rapidly cooling temperature. She stopped herself from following, and on impulse headed into the bedroom. She hadn't checked on her mother since leaving St Lucia, and for some unknown reason she felt her heart lodge in her throat as she dialled her number.

She hadn't decided when to tell her mother about her inheritance. They hadn't spoken about Luigi, the man she'd been so briefly married to, in years, and Faye wondered sometimes if her mother had succeeded in forgetting him. Regardless of that, Faye knew she'd have to tell her eventually.

The call crackled, and when her mother came on the line it grew progressively patchy. Eventually Faye gave up, with a promise to call back, and looked up to find Maceo leaning in the doorway. Even though she'd revealed her darkest secrets to him, she still tensed. Had he overheard her conversation?

'I didn't mean to disturb you,' she said, trying to read his face.

He shrugged. 'I came to suggest you wait until the storm is over because the connection will be bad.'

She nodded. 'I sort of got that.'

His gaze dropped to her phone. 'How was your mother?'

Her tension increased. 'I couldn't really tell. I'm hoping she's the same as when we spoke in St Lucia.'

His eyes narrowed. 'What's her general state?'

Pain lanced through her. 'She has good days and bad days.' It was an adequate enough answer. And yet she found herself elaborating. 'The assault was traumatic in itself, but the real trauma came when she found out she was carrying me. I think that completely broke her mentally. I was oblivious to her deep trauma for years before she got help.'

He walked into the room, his hands leaving his pockets to hang by his sides. 'You were a child. How could you have known?'

'I was old enough to see how hard she took Luigi's leaving. She got so bad we were both assigned counsellors. I was too young to grasp exactly what was going on half the time, but I knew that she was suffering. About a year after Luigi left her counsellor suggested New Paths as a permanent residence. It was a whole new experience for her. Most of the time she thrives there, but every now and then she has a relapse.'

Maceo flinched and his expression turned almost furious. Just as he had on the balcony, he turned away abruptly.

Her stomach hollowed. 'Sorry if that was TMI. Not everyone wants to know the messy details.'

He turned back to her, his eyes burning. 'On the contrary. I want to know everything.'

The firm assurance brought a lump to her throat. Swallowing, she nodded. 'New Paths has a high success rate with alternative therapies. Mum's is a combination of medication, art and music therapy, specifically designed for her. That's the kind of therapy I want to do eventually,' she confessed quietly.

Enlightenment fired in his eyes. 'That's what you intend to use your inheritance for?'

'Yes,' she stated boldly. 'You probably think it's not—'

'I think it's highly commendable. Luigi would be proud.'

Tears prickled at her eyes. 'Do you think so?'

He nodded, his eyes gentling in a way that suggested he wasn't as unaffected as she'd imagined. They stared at one another, jagged understanding throbbing between them. Then another crack of thunder attempted to shatter the tree house.

She jumped. Maceo chuckled.

The atmosphere was broken. And when he returned to his desk a minute later Faye couldn't help but accept that she'd slipped just a little bit further down that slippery road where her heart was in even more danger.

CHAPTER TEN

IT WAS A little terrifying how returning to Capri felt to Faye like coming home. Perhaps the feeling stemmed from never having had a true home, her mother's mental fragility and resulting anxiety having left her in a state of flux.

Those two years spent with Luigi had been her closest to stability and 'home'…

Pico's over-exuberant greeting merely deepened the sensation of homecoming. And that night, when he scratched at the door for entry into Maceo's bedroom—where he'd insisted she moved—she smiled at Maceo's put-upon expression.

'I'm under no illusion that he's pining for me,' he said.

'Will you let him in, please?'

'I suspect I'll have to—or else listen to him whine all night,' he growled, before rising to open the door.

A thoroughly pleased Pico rushed in, but when he attempted to jump onto the bed Maceo whistled sharply. 'He can stay for tonight, but I refuse to have him on our bed.'

Her heart squeezed, then banged against her ribs in foolish reaction to his words. Under the guise of petting Pico, Faye ruthlessly tried to bring her feelings under control. Which turned out to be a futile task because, a moment later, when Maceo tugged her into his arms, the cascade of emotion smashed her fortitude to smithereens.

In the following weeks Maceo continued to whittle away at her foundations until Faye accepted that when she eventually left she would be taking an extra suitcase full of heartache with her. Because her feelings for Maceo had long passed the *just sex* they were supposed to be indulging in.

To stop herself being totally overcome by her staggering emotions, she attempted to place a professional distance between them—first by requesting a return to the R&D department, and then by demanding that they keep their physical relationship between themselves.

Maceo grumbled, but when she refused to back down, after a twenty-minute debate, he grudgingly gave in, before pulling her beneath him in bed with the instruction to put him in a better mood—a task Faye was all too delighted to perform.

Day after day, she was discovering tiny new facets of her lover.

Maceo could be gentle when required, was extremely generous to his staff, and without fail, visited his family's memorial every weekend.

On the third weekend after their return she asked to accompany him. He hesitated for a fraction of a second before holding out his hand.

An hour later she stood beside him, tears prickling in her eyes as she paid her respects to the only father she'd ever known, silently accepting that she would never truly know all the answers.

There was one question she hadn't yet asked, though.

She tried to ignore the lingering distance she felt from Maceo as they left the cemetery. But, just as when they'd been in St Lucia, she felt that small pebble of unease chafe, its presence looming larger with each day.

'I've never asked about Pietro's whereabouts… I'm assuming the two of you aren't in touch?'

Maceo stiffened, and the hand gripping hers tightened. 'No,' he said tersely.

He said nothing more. Faye pulled at his hand till he stopped. Looking into his face, she glimpsed a caginess she'd never witnessed before.

'Maceo, what is it?'

His lips thinned and his jaw clenched before he answered. 'He died of a drug overdose in Malaysia, three years ago.'

She gasped, her gaze swinging back to the family mausoleum. Maceo shook his head. 'He left instructions to be cremated wherever he died. I didn't attend the funeral.'

He resumed walking and after a moment she joined him, aware that the distance between them was widening. But she was leaving in a few weeks. Reminded of how Luigi had left her with questions, Faye swore she wouldn't let Maceo do the same.

* * *

They had no dinner plans the following Friday, and, as had become her habit, when she finished work she took the lift to Maceo's floor.

Bruno was nowhere in sight. About to knock on his door, she hesitated when she heard voices.

With a grimace, she lowered her hand, recognising Stefano's and Francesco's cold tones. She'd stayed clear of them since the party at Villa Serenita, and wondered about why Maceo kept them around, considering the obvious friction between them.

She shrugged mentally. Luigi and Maceo's parents had accommodated Pietro, despite his deplorable behaviour. It stood to reason Carlotta would do the same for her brothers.

About to retreat, and wait for Maceo in one of the conference rooms, Faye froze when she heard her name. She knew she shouldn't eavesdrop, but a need to overcame her better judgement.

After several weeks in Italy she'd picked up enough Italian words to grasp the gist of a conversation, although she didn't have to be fluent to recognise the brothers' tone.

'The little whore...'

'Paparazzi sniffing around...'

'Perhaps they need to be indulged...'

Maceo's terse response produced a chilling silence she could feel even from behind the closed door. Both brothers snarled something right before she heard footsteps. She tried to retreat, but didn't get far enough. The door flew open and twin pairs of beady eyes glared at her.

Behind them, Maceo stood tall and furious. His gaze gentled a touch when he saw her, but he turned away almost immediately, raking his fingers through his hair as he strode to the window.

She entered his office, shutting the door behind her. 'Everything all right?'

'No.'

'May I ask what that was about?'

He tensed visibly, fingers massaging his nape. 'Leave it.'

She hadn't expected the harsh answer. Cold dread slithered through her stomach. 'Is it about how they treated Carlotta? Shouldn't you let that go, Maceo?' she urged softly.

He spun around, his eyes flames of rage. 'No. Because they're *snakes*. At every turn they try to undermine my position.'

'Can't you just vote them off the board?'

His jaw tightened. 'I might be the majority shareholder but I don't have the ultimate overruling authority. Not yet, anyway.'

She frowned. What she'd overheard had sounded personal. About *her*. 'So what was it about just now?' she pressed.

She sensed his withdrawal, saw the shutters coming down before he turned to his desk. 'They're making their usual threats. Wanting something for nothing.'

Perhaps it wasn't a lie, but she suspected it wasn't the whole story either. But, really, was it her business when he was visibly freezing her out?

'I'm ready to leave,' she said, changing the subject. 'I can go ahead if you want?' she suggested, hoping he'd refuse. Hoping he'd snap out of his mood so things could return to normal. But what was normal when the clock was counting down until this thing reached its end date?

'We will leave together,' he stated gruffly.

But even as he gathered his files, strode towards her and took her hand, he was a thousand miles away.

Dinner was a stilted affair, his thoughts clearly elsewhere. But all that changed when they reached the bedroom. There he focused his full attention on her. And, like the fool she was, she surrendered, allowed his searing passion to burn away her chaotic thoughts.

For a week they carried on in the same vein. Then came the added concern of her mother's suddenly frequent contact, in which she demanded to know when Faye would be returning.

Assuring her that she would return soon only highlighted how close she was to leaving Capri.

How close she was to walking away from the man she suspected she'd fallen in love with.

When her mother's calls increased in frequency the next day, Faye was forced to consider cutting her time even shorter. Perhaps going home to see her mother. Her heart eased a little at the thought that she didn't have to leave permanently just yet. She would just fly home for a couple of days.

Deciding to tell Maceo, she left her favourite position beside the pool, where she'd been toying with more new flavour combinations.

It was Saturday, but Maceo was working at home.

The first thing she noticed was the staff's tension as she passed them in the hallway.

Her second discovery was Maceo's absence from his study.

The reason for the staff's tension became clear when she heard Maceo's furious voice and saw his angry pacing a moment later as he crossed the terrace outside.

She was debating whether to retreat when her gaze fell on the papers strewn on his desk. Nausea congealed in her stomach as she saw the first of the shrieking headlines. Then the one after that. All with accompanying pictures.

One picture was of her leaving the cemetery with Maceo. Another was of him clutching her hand as they raced towards his helicopter. A third grainy one showed them on his beach in St Lucia, clenched in a lovers' embrace that left no doubt as to their relationship.

But it was the lurid revealing headlines that rammed horror down her throat. That filled every atom of her being with utter desolation until a hoarse cry left her throat and her knees gave way.

Billionaire CEO Dates Child of Rape!
In Bed with the Dirty Laundry!

She slapped her hand over her mouth, as if that would stop the sickening feeling cascading through her. Firm hands grabbed her, attempted to right her. With a horrified shriek, she pushed Maceo away.

'Faye...' His voice was low, imploring.

She staggered away from him. As she did so her hip bumped his desk, sending papers flying to the ground. She started to reach for them but Maceo surged forward.

'Leave them!'

The peculiar note in his voice froze her. Growing colder, she peered more closely at the papers she'd dislodged. It was a report of some sort. And within the long script several familiar names jumped out at her. Hers. Her mother's. *New Paths. Luigi. Pietro?*

'Maceo, what is this?' Her shaking voice echoed her devastated soul.

His lips thinned, highlighting the whiteness around his mouth, his ashen pallor. '*Per favore.* Leave it, Faye,' he urged, his tone cajoling in a way that rattled her even more.

'No. I won't leave it. Why are you investigating me?'

'I don't want to do it like this.'

'Do what?' she shrieked. '*Tell* me!' When he didn't answer, she pointed to the newspapers. 'Did you do this?'

Anger restored his colour. 'Of course not.'

'Then who did? You're the only one who—'

'Do not even finish that sentence.'

But her pain seared too deep. 'Why not? I told Matt what happened to my mother, but this level of detail… No one knows that but you.'

Maceo's fury evaporated, leaving behind thick censure that added to the dread crawling through her.

'And you automatically assume I would betray you?'

'I don't know!'

'You should!' he sliced at her.

'Why? Because we're sleeping together?' She lashed out, her pain too huge to contain.

A look almost of hurt crossed his face before it hardened into a rigid mask. 'Because I told you I would always be straight with you.'

'Then explain why you're investigating me.'

'I'm not investigating you. I'm investigating Pietro. And Luigi.'

'Why?'

For a tight stretch he remained silent. Then, with a bleak look, he shook his head. 'Because I don't think Luigi's arrival in your mother's life was un-planned.'

Her vision wavered. She clutched the side of the desk to keep upright.

'What...?'

But she *knew*. Like a snake slithering in the dark towards her, the poisonous truth was about to sting. Change her life for ever.

'Luigi went to England purposely to find your mother—and you.'

'Explain, Maceo,' she pleaded, aware that her lips had gone numb. Her whole body had gone numb. Only a tiny sliver of her brain worked.

'Because he suspected your mother's attacker was Pietro. And in his own way he wanted to make things right.'

The sting arrived like a hot lance to her heart. Vaguely she was aware that she was shaking her head, that every atom in her being was shaking in denial. Just as she was aware that Maceo had dropped to his knees before her and was staring at her with eyes that pitied her.

'No!' she snarled.

He lowered his head, his shoulders heaving. 'Yes.'

'Oh, my God. He lied to me,' she whispered. '*You* lied to me. About everything.'

'*No.*' The word was raw, gravel-rough. 'No,' he repeated. 'I was gathering facts. I needed to be sure before—'

'Before you splashed my family's sordid dirty laundry all over the papers?'

'That wasn't my doing. It was Francesco and Stefano. I had no idea they were doing some digging of their own. What you overheard in my office… they were attempting to blackmail me—'

'And you let them? So you could keep me onside until you got your hands on that precious share?'

His nostrils flared and she knew she'd hit the mark.

'You did, didn't you? Your precious company is worth more to you than…than anything else.' She barely stopped herself from saying *than me*.

'To have ultimate control of the company, I need to be a one hundred per cent shareholder. That's why I can't get rid of them. And yes, this isn't how I would've gone about dealing with your news. But it's not the end of the world.'

She laughed—a grating sound that frightened her. 'It's easy to say that when you're the golden child of parents who loved each other and loved you. You have *no earthly idea* what I feel.'

'Perhaps not. But that doesn't mean you should let this define you.'

'What do you expect me to do? Walk out into the street and own it?'

To her utter shock and dismay, he nodded.

'*Si.* Take the power away from them. Turn this into a positive.'

'God, you're actually serious! Do you have *any*

idea how this will affect my mother?' Fresh horror shrouded her. 'Oh, God. My mother!'

He rose and held out his phone. 'Call her.'

'And say what? That I trusted the wrong person with the most devastating thing to happen to her?'

His fingers tightened around the phone. 'I will not persistently defend myself. If you won't call your mother, how will you know she's okay?'

'How do you think? By going home to her!'

He frowned. 'What are you saying?'

'That I'm leaving! Surely you can't expect me to stay here after this?'

To her chagrin, he looked utterly stunned. She walked towards the door, her feet blocks of concrete.

'Faye.'

She didn't stop. She was terrified she would break down if she did. And she refused to leave Maceo with the memory of seeing her completely defeated.

'Faye, wait. There's something else.'

Misery drenched her. There couldn't be. She knew without a shadow of a doubt that she wouldn't be able to take it. But she couldn't move. Because even drowning in utter desolation she still held out the hope of something from him. Something that resembled a reciprocal feeling of that precious knot of longing inside her that had somehow survived these devastating revelations.

Something like…hope.

Like *love*.

She held her breath as he approached. But when he arrived beside her he didn't arrive with words. Instead, he held out an envelope. One with her name on it.

Confused, she lifted her gaze to his.

'Carlotta left this for you. It's from Luigi,' he said.

Hope dissolved into despair and Faye couldn't even find the strength to be angry. 'Another lie?' she rasped.

'No. But I didn't think you were in a frame of mind to hear the truth before.'

'That's how you intend to justify withholding this from me?'

His jaw clenched. 'This is how you choose to end things, Faye? With accusations?'

'I didn't end this, Maceo. You did.'

Slowly that formidable façade locked in, his statue-like hauteur erasing every trace of emotion from his face.

'Go, then. Don't let me stop you.'

She snatched the letter. And left.

Maceo stood in one corner of the conference room, attempting to block out the buzz of excitement growing steadily behind him. Casa di Fiorenti hadn't had a new product launch in two years. It stood to reason his shareholders were thrilled at the prospect of a new range.

Alberto and his team had pulled out all the stops to preview the Arcobaleno range in only six short weeks. His ambition to push it through production in time for Christmas was well on track too.

Maceo didn't care. These days he cared very little about anything. Except for the excruciating passage of time.

Six weeks.

A lifetime since she walked out of his study. He'd laboured under the misapprehension that relocating to his office at his Rome headquarters might solve the problem of seeing her face around every corner—that returning to his penthouse apartment in the heart of his favourite city might erase the memories of her that haunted Villa Serenita.

But no.

Everywhere he went he saw her.

His staff offered pitying looks while his employees scurried away when they saw him coming. And why shouldn't they? He was intolerable to be around.

Not even the satisfaction of pushing his lawyers to find the loophole that had enabled him to finally toss Carlotta's brothers off the board had eased the savage ache inside him.

Several times he reached for the phone. Each time he lost his nerve.

Maceo laughed under his breath. He'd been through a car accident, a coma, months of intense rehabilitation, only to be cowed by the rejection of a diminutive woman with rainbow colours in her hair?

Arcobaleno.

His insides twisted at the name that suited her from head to toe. He was certain he wouldn't be able to see another rainbow without being reminded of Faye.

Should he have stopped her from leaving? How could he when she was right?

He'd withheld crucial information about who she was. He'd devastated her as surely as his own parents had devastated him. And so soon after she'd delivered him from his dark torment. For that alone he deserved this suffering.

'*Signor...?*' Alberto addressed him hesitantly. 'They're waiting for you to make a speech.'

Too bad. He was fresh out of congratulatory speeches. The only talking he wanted to do was to the woman who'd left an indelible mark on him. The woman without whom he was beginning to fear he would perish and fade away to nothing.

He stared into the glass of vintage champagne he hadn't touched, attempting to summon words that held genuine meaning. Each one felt flat and false. Hell, even the weather was conspiring against him.

In the square below, tourists milled about, huddled together or seeking shelter from the sudden downpour that had caught them unawares. Like him, they'd expected sunshine, only to be greeted with grey clouds.

He lifted his gaze, glared at the clouds. Just then they parted. By the smallest fraction. But it was enough to let through a stream of sunshine. And within that sunshine…

Maceo's heart tripped over as he caught sight of the faintest rainbow.

He didn't believe in that sort of foolishness. Yet he couldn't take his eyes off the colourful arc.

A tremor moved through him. Turning, he shoved his drink into Alberto's startled hands.

'You make the speech. You brought this to fruition.'

'It wasn't just me,' Alberto replied, a sombre look in his eyes.

Maceo nod grimly. 'No, it wasn't. And I should do something about that, no?'

Alberto was smiling as Maceo strode out of his own meeting, totally uncaring of the stunned looks he received as he walked out.

For the first time in endless weeks purpose flowed through his veins.

'Are you going to mope today as well?'

Faye looked up, startled, from the book she'd been half-heartedly reading.

'Excuse me?'

Her mother set her teacup down. 'I may be a little loopy, but I'm not stupid.'

'You're not loopy, Mum. Please stop saying that.'

Her mother gave her a sad little smile. 'We both know what I am, Faye.'

'Mum…'

Her mother reached across the small table where they were having tea and laid a hand on her arm. 'It's fine, sweetheart. You don't need to say it. You never need to say it.'

Tears that hovered just beneath the surface of Faye's emotions rose. Rapidly she blinked them away. 'I'm not sure what you're talking about.'

'You check your phone a hundred times a day. You perk up when the postman arrives and wither when he leaves you empty-handed.'

Faye started to protest, but her mother wasn't finished.

'That letter you keep in your pocket and read a dozen times a day when you think I'm not looking…'

Faye's mouth dropped open.

Her mother smiled. 'I'm not stupid,' she repeated softly.

A tear escaped.

Her mother brushed it away. 'Tell me,' she invited.

So Faye told her. About Carlotta's initial contact. About Luigi's bequest. Selectively about Maceo. Even about Matt, at which her mother echoed Maceo's words so eerily, her heart lurched.

'He's a deplorable human being. Don't waste another moment's thought on him.'

But when she reached the hardest part she stopped. 'I can't, Mum…'

'It's something to do with what happened to me, isn't it?'

Miserable, Faye nodded. Then the words came tumbling out.

An apology for how she'd come into the world was written in the pages of Luigi's letter. In it, he admitted his knowledge of what his brother had done to her mother—how, several years after the attack, a family friend who'd attended the same party had divulged what he suspected had happened.

Luigi, ever the conscientious brother, had looked further into the incident and tracked down her mother. His discovery that Angela had borne his brother's child had shocked him. He'd intended to make anonymous reparation, but then he'd seen Angela with Faye in a playground.

Befriending Angela had revealed to Luigi the true depths of her fragile mental state. He'd married her out of guilt, and a desperate need to make amends, but had known deep down he couldn't provide the sort of care Angela needed. Steering her to New Paths had been his way of helping her after he'd fallen in love with Carlotta. He had always been ashamed he'd never revealed his true identity and he begged forgiveness.

Faye's discovery that her school scholarship had been orchestrated by Luigi, and that New Paths was fully funded by a Fiorenti-Caprio foundation, had enraged her for all of five minutes before she'd dissolved into tears again. Luigi had done his best for them, and she couldn't fault him for that.

'I don't think I can quite bring myself to say his name, but I'm glad you have the answers you need,' her mother said, her eyes a forest of shadows.

It was Faye's turn to comfort her. 'I'm so sorry, Mum.'

Her mother nodded solemnly. 'I know he left us, but I'm glad you had a father figure for a while— especially when I couldn't be the mother you deserved.'

A lump clogged Faye's throat. 'I wouldn't trade you for the world.'

They stayed silent, absorbing their emotions.

'Now, the postman…' Angela pressed. 'What's that about?'

Faye blinked away fresh tears. Since her email account remained empty of anything to do with Maceo or Casa di Fiorenti, she'd taken to stalking the postman. She knew she should give up now, after six weeks of silence, and instruct a lawyer to deal with securing her inheritance. Except her inheritance wasn't paramount in her mind. What she yearned for more was something, *anything*, from the man she'd lost her heart to in Naples. Even if it was a stuffy letter from his legal team.

'You're holding back about this Maceo. Is he the one?' her mother intuited.

Faye's heart quaked even when she thought about him. 'Yes.'

'What happened?'

Misery gripped her tight. Miraculously, those harrowing tabloid exposés hadn't reached Devon. Faye intended to keep it that way.

'We rowed… I accused him of…of unspeakable things.'

'Did he deserve it?'

Faye held her breath for the longest time, then shook her head. 'I didn't wait for an explanation.'

'I suspect you *know* he didn't deserve it, or you wouldn't be feeling this bad.'

Tears of remorse slid down her cheeks as she accepted her mother's assessment. Shock and pain had stopped her from hearing Maceo out. From accepting his reasons for withholding. Six weeks of silence said she'd lost her chance.

'You may be in luck today. Here's the postman.'

Faye twisted in her seat, her heart hammering as the middle-aged man made a beeline for her. He pulled out a thick envelope and handed it over. Transfixed, she stared at the Casa di Fiorenti logo.

'Is this what you're waiting for?' her mother asked.

Was it?

Swallowing, she tore the letter open, devouring the missive from Maceo's lawyers, offering to buy her share. If she agreed to the sum, the formal signing would be in London in two days. If she didn't agree, she was welcome to commence negotiations with Maceo via his lawyers.

Despite her heart sinking at the stiff formality of the letter, her insides continued to somersault. Would Maceo be in London?

Even without knowing the answer Faye knew she would be there.

Taking a deep breath, she read the rest of the document. Her mouth dropped open when she saw how much Maceo intended to offer her. It was almost twice what his lawyers in Naples had said the partial share was worth. Whether Maceo turned up or not, she would be a fool to reject it.

She looked up. Her mother was smiling.

'Regardless of how you came into the world, you deserve every happiness. You've settled your past, Faye. Now go and fight for your future.'

Fighting more tears, Faye leaned over and kissed her mother. Then she rose from the table.

She was going to London.

Maceo clenched his fists, impatience bristling through him as he paced his living room. He was reduced to voyeurism—a silent participant watching Faye via the monitor in his penthouse while his lawyers took their sweet time securing her signature.

He'd given them carte blanche to offer her whatever she wanted, but evidently his instruction that the transaction should be conducted in the shortest possible time hadn't quite sunk in.

He was half a second from picking up the phone when they finished. The moment they left, Bruno escorted Faye to the lift. Maceo was waiting when the doors parted on the penthouse floor thirty seconds later.

She was facing away from him, wearing a coral concoction, with bangles to match and a similar colour threaded through her hair, and he welcomed the much-needed moment to compose himself.

Then she turned, her breath catching when she saw him. *Mio Dio*, she was beautiful.

'Maceo! I thought you weren't… What am I doing up here?'

'I wish to talk to you.'

'Then why weren't you downstairs with your lawyers?'

Because I'm a damn mess.

'Because I didn't want business to muddle this.'

'And what is *"this"*, exactly?' she enquired, raising her chin.

'Would you like to come in? *Per favore,*' he pleaded.

Her gaze flicked past him into the penthouse and Maceo caught the slightest wobble in her chin. It was the tiniest chink in her armour, but he found himself praying it was a sign that all wasn't lost.

She walked past him, head held high. He followed, his heart racing as her alluring scent reminded him of its absence on his pillow.

She reached the sofa and turned to face him. 'Tell me why I'm here.'

'Because, my beautiful rainbow, I'm a desperate man, here to plead my case,' he stated baldly.

She reached out blindly, clutched the back of the sofa.

Maceo exhaled, his prayers intensifying. She wasn't immune to him.

'We said everything we had to say to one another in Italy,' she said.

'Did we? Are you absolutely certain I can't say more?'

'Depends on what the subject matter is.'

Unable to keep his distance, he took a few steps towards her. She didn't retreat. Another mercy.

'You were right, *cara*.'

'About…?' she queried, her eyes filming with a pain he would give his limbs to erase.

'About how I handled everything. Regardless of my feelings on the matter, I should've given you the information you needed for your own closure. My conceit made me believe mine was the right way. I hurt you, Faye. And I'm here to say…*mi dispiace*. I am also here to make amends.'

Something close to disappointment crossed her face. 'Is that all you're here for?'

'No,' he said. 'I am a greedy man who wants more. Much more.'

She gripped the sofa harder. 'Then perhaps this time you shouldn't quit while you're ahead?'

The thread of hope in her voice triggered his. He ventured even closer, heard her breath catch in the softest gasp. With every fibre of his being he yearned to hold her.

'I've missed you, Faye. Desperately.'

Her nostrils quivered but she remained silent.

He took that as his cue to risk everything. 'I held back about Pietro because I was ashamed. I've been ashamed of what Luigi and my parents did to cover up his activities for a very long time. Even after you showed me that there was a way forward, there was still shame. My family was responsible for letting him get away with his depravities. When you showed me his picture on the yacht, I couldn't dismiss the possibility that he was connected to you somehow. You obviously take after your mother, since you look nothing like him, but I couldn't tell you until I was absolutely certain.'

To his utter relief, she nodded. 'I was upset when I found out what you did, but eventually I understood the reasoning behind it.'

Relief smashed harder through him. 'About the letter... Carlotta made me promise to hold on to it for at least three months before giving it you.'

'Why?'

'I suspect she was hoping that what happened between us would happen. That I would meet you, see how special you are and perhaps in time it would not be too late for me. That this thing living within me now would take hold.'

She stopped breathing and her eyes latched onto his. 'What is the thing living inside you, Maceo?'

Her beautiful voice was hardly above a murmur.

'It is the need for you that never goes away. The desire to be with you every hour of every day, to make you smile, to hear you laugh, to plan a future with you by my side, bearing our children, growing old with me. It is this love I have inside for you, *amore mio*. Carlotta was an eternal optimist and I will be in her debt for ever.'

'Why?'

'Because she brought you to me. I mentioned the vow I made over my parents' grave?'

She nodded.

He reached into his pocket. 'They made a list, mapping out their lives from the night they got engaged to their old age. I was number two, right after their wedding. Casa di Fiorenti was number five. There are eighteen things on that list, Faye.' His fingers closed over the paper, pain rippling through him. 'They only made it to number seven. Because of me.'

She gave a choked cry. 'Oh… Maceo…'

'So I vowed to deprive myself of the happiness I robbed them of.'

'No… They wouldn't have wanted that for you, Maceo,' she said.

'I see that now, *amore*. You came along and I was happy to fail. Because you opened my eyes and my heart to a life beyond accumulating wealth and solitude and sacrifice. What is it all worth without someone to share it? Now I've had time to look at this list in a different light, and I can do everything in here *for* them. I know they loved me enough to wish it so. And even if I don't get to cross off the last item, and die in your arms, what I experienced with you during our time together will be enough.'

'Wow… You're giving up so easily?' she taunted, but her eyes shone bright.

Maceo laughed. 'Never. This is simply an initial skirmish. I'm Italian. I will pursue you relentlessly. Desire anything in the world and it will be yours, *tesoro*. Even Pico. Who misses you dreadfully.'

She smiled. Then sobered. 'I miss him too. But what if the only thing I truly want in the world is you?'

His world shifted beneath his feet, then righted itself in a way that made him want to shout with joy.

'What then, Maceo?' she pressed.

'Then you will have me,' he vowed on a shaken breath. 'Immediately. Now.'

Her face transformed, blooming with a smile he knew he would never forget as long as he lived. She swayed towards him and Maceo closed the gap between them, sweeping her off her feet as the sun burst through the clouds.

He froze, his gaze darting to the skies.

'What are you looking for?' she asked.

When what he searched for didn't appear, Maceo knew why. Staring into the face of the woman who held his heart, he felt joy overflow within him.

'Nothing, *amore mio*. I search for nothing. Because everything I want is right here in my arms.'

Tears filmed her eyes. 'I love you, Maceo. So much.'

Gently, he brushed her tears away. *'Ti amo anch'io, il mio bellisimmo arcobaleno.'*

Her smile widened. 'I love it when you call me that.'

'Then you should come with me back to Italy. There's a wonderful surprise waiting for you.'

The new Arcobaleno range of specially flavoured chocolates shaped like rainbows had been her idea. Maceo intended it to be one of many projects he undertook with her.

'I will follow you anywhere, my love.'

'That's good to hear. Because right now I would very much love you to come with me to the bedroom. I have six weeks to make up for, plus a lifetime.'

'I will—right after you show me that list.'

He handed it over, watched her face as she read it, then raised her beautiful face to his.

'Can we start from the beginning and work our way through it?' she asked.

A lump clogged his throat. 'As long as I get to shower you with love, live each day with you and die in your arms, you have a deal.'

Her smile filled his heart. 'I accept.'

And in that moment Maceo swore that he would never cause her to be without that smile.

* * * * *

Adored The Commanding Italian's Challenge?
*You're sure to enjoy these
other Maya Blake stories!*

The Sicilian's Banished Bride
Kidnapped for His Royal Heir
Bound by My Scandalous Pregnancy
Claiming My Hidden Son

Available now!